not so SUDDENLY SOULMATES

NOT SO UNHAPPILY EVER AFTER #1

A NEW ADULT ROMANTIC COMEDY

<h1 style="text-align:center">Books by Ellen Wilder</h1>

NOT SO UNHAPPILY EVER AFTER

Not So Suddenly Soulmates

THE VITALLI FAMILY SAGA

Nothing Without You

Moments With You (*previously titled Stolen Moments*)

Stay With You (*previously titled Stay*)

ROMANCING ROSE COUNTY

Escape to Rose County (novella)

LOVE GROWS WILD

Love Blossoms (An LGW Duology #1 w/Amber Root)

Love Blooms (An LGW Duology #2 w/Amber Root)

With Love, Dakota and Carter

not so SUDDENLY SOULMATES

NOT SO UNHAPPILY EVER AFTER # 1

A NEW ADULT ROMANTIC COMEDY

ELLEN WILDER

About Not So Suddenly Soulmates

Rhi Edgerly has never been one for long-term relationships—occasional flings and on-again, off-again boyfriends more than enough for her. But with her twenty-fifth birthday on the horizon, she finds the thrill wearing off and is toying with the idea of something more serious. But the only one she can imagine spending her life with is her roommate and lifelong best friend, Levi.

Between his demanding tech job, a never-ending string of one-night stands, and regular party host duties, confirmed bachelor Levi Morris is getting tired. His job feels like a chore and he finds himself just going through the motions with everyone but Rhi. When a killer job opportunity lands in his lap, he has to decide whether he wants to stay with Rhi in Indianapolis or move back home to Bryton.

Rhi and Levi know they'll be friends for the rest of their lives. But after a few bad dates, an almost kiss, and a new job two hours away, will they risk their almost twenty year friendship to see what kind of soulmates they truly are?

Not So Suddenly Soulmates is a friends-to-lovers new adult rom-com with a lot of laughs, plenty of eye rolls, and a little bit of island vacation heat. This stand-alone book is set in the Then Came Love world from Ellen Wilder and Amber Root.

To my kids,
who will never read it because, and I quote,
"Who wants to read a book with sex in it?"

And to my husband,
who wrote one of my editor's favorite lines in the book.

Chapter One

Rhi

May 5th

A piercing scream pulled Rhi Edgerly out of a dead sleep. Tangled in her comforter, she tumbled out of bed and hit the floor with a thud. Rhi surveyed her surroundings. "What the f—"

"Ohmigod! What was that?" a woman shouted from the other room.

Rhi growled as she extracted herself from the blanket. "Yes, Levi. I just *love* being woken up on a Saturday morning by another one of your exploits," she mumbled.

"Shh. It's my roommate."

Rhi shook her head, stood, and put the comforter on her bed.

"Roommate? I didn't know you had a roommate."

Bingo.

"She should be up any moment." Levi's voice grew a notch sarcastic—their agreed-upon sign he was on his way to her room. "Rhi *loves* to meet my girlfriends." He knocked on the door.

"Fuck you," she shouted as she reached for her robe. *Damn. This girl's getting clingy already?* She checked her cell phone on the nightstand and groaned. *Six-thirty? I just fell asleep.*

"A girl? You have a *girl* for a roommate?"

She tied her robe and walked to the door.

"What? It's not like we sleep together or anything."

Rhi opened her door and smacked her best friend in the arm before making her way into the kitchen. "You wish, Levi Morris."

Levi cringed.

Payback is a bitch. Wake me up early, and they'll know your last name. She trudged to the counter and rolled her eyes when she noticed the empty coffee pot. "The least you could do, if you're going to be screaming on a Saturday morning, is make coffee." She held the carafe out toward her roommate.

"Sorry. You know I like it better when you make it." He came up behind her and bent down so his mouth was close to her ear. "Get her out of here fast. Once and she's already brought up the 'L-word.'" He snatched the pot from Rhi's hand and placed it on the counter.

Rhi pushed him away. "I don't like her. The last person I want to have a threesome with is someone who screams as loud as she does."

"Come on, Rhi. She got scared when you fell out of bed." He flashed a toothy grin.

She fought a smile and drew a line in the air with her hands. "Dude. *She* screamed and made *me* fall out of bed. Not. Going. To. Happen."

The blonde shook her head, causing her messy curls to bounce. "Wait, what? I'm not into girls at all."

"Good, 'cause I'm not into you—at all." Rhi turned around and reached for the bag of coffee in the cabinet.

"Look at her. She's the perfect height and good in bed too. I tried her out for you." Levi leaned back against the counter, one foot crossed over the other.

Rhi glanced at Levi, thankful he took the time to put on a pair of jeans. "Of course you did." She rubbed her temples then turned around to stare at the other woman, giving her a once-over. "She's blonde. I don't like blondes."

"You *tried me out*? You brought me here for a threesome with your roommate?" The blonde planted her hands on her hips, and her lower lip quivered.

"He chose wrong. *Very* wrong." Rhi kicked his foot as she walked past him.

"Ouch, what was that for?"

Rhi shook her head and grabbed the woman's hand. "You wanna go to breakfast and talk about it?"

The blonde jumped back as if she'd been burned. "N-no."

Rhi growled, opened the front door, and shoved the woman and her shoes out into the hallway. "There was no threesome. He's just not into you. Have a nice day." She slammed the door in the woman's face, marched back to the coffee pot, and filled her mug.

Levi laughed. "You usually don't get bored."

Rhi glowered at him. "It's six-thirty on a Saturday. I barely made it into bed by three, and I was rudely awakened by a woman screaming, causing me to fall out of bed."

"Let me make it up to you. I'll take you out to

breakfast." Levi grabbed a mug and poured himself some coffee, offering to top Rhi's off before he set the carafe down again.

She quirked a brow over her cup. "Somewhere expensive that serves mimosas?"

"Somewhere cheap that has orange juice." Levi watched their grey tabby cat jump onto the counter then reached out to stroke the cat's fur. "You need a bath, Duke."

The cat growled, leaped to the floor, and sauntered away.

"He hates baths." Rhi sipped her coffee. "I believe I still have Jamie's number saved in my phone. I'd be more than happy to call her and tell her how much you *loooove* her." She set her mug down on the counter, got the creamer from the fridge, and splashed some in her mug. "You bought the cheap shit again."

"You know I hate grocery shopping." Levi folded his arms over his chest. "And you wouldn't dare."

"We order groceries online and they're usually here in a few hours. Just tell me when we're out." Rhi pulled her phone out of her pocket and scanned through the names until she found Jamie's number. She held her finger over the call button and tilted her screen so he could see she wasn't bluffing. "You wanna bet?"

"Bellerose Café?"

Rhi nodded and closed her contacts list. "Plus, you'll add what we need to the grocery app or text me when we're out. Then we have a deal."

"I deleted that app months ago. We've lived together for five years. Have I ever remembered to tell you when we need things?" He kissed her cheek. "Thanks for helping out."

Rhi returned the gesture and let out a sigh. "How you'll ever live on your own is beyond me." She pulled her robe tighter and scurried into her bedroom.

"You'll never leave me." Levi followed and perched on the side of her bed.

"It could happen." She walked to her closet and scanned her clothes. *Why did I choose gourmet food? I can't get away with yoga pants and a T-shirt at Bellerose.* "We could each find that perfect person and get married...or at least want to live with that person."

"Bachelor." Levi pointed at himself with his thumb. "Lifelong bachelor, remember?"

"You slept with Jamie twice." She picked a navy wrap dress with white flowers. *What would I do if Levi does find that special someone someday?*

"Are you ever gonna quit teasing me about that?"

"Nope." Rhi stepped out of her closet and turned around in front of him. "Good enough for Bellerose?"

"Perfect. Except you can't go barefoot." Levi winked at her. "I'll get dressed and meet you at the car."

She wadded up a piece of paper from her desk and threw it at him as he darted out of her room. She slipped on a pair of navy ballet flats and a lightweight gray cardigan before grabbing her purse and heading through the apartment to the front door.

"Hey. You just getting home too?"

Rhi pulled the door shut and turned toward their neighbor, taking a moment to look at his bloodshot eyes, messy hair, and half-buttoned dress shirt. "Hey, Robby. Levi and I are going to Bellerose. Are you okay?"

Robby nodded. "Levi dumped the blonde this early?" He took a step closer and draped his arm over her shoulders.

She wriggled out of his embrace and moved toward the stairs. *Boundaries, dude. I'll get you to learn what that means someday.* "Like Levi ever dumps any of them. I had to do it." She reached into her purse for her phone and quickly texted Levi.

RHI:

Hurry up. Robby just got home and is hungover.

Robby squinted at his watch. "It's only seven. She must have been an early riser."

"More like an early screamer," Rhi grumbled.

The apartment door opened, and Levi strode out dressed in black pants and a maroon dress shirt, the top three buttons undone.

"Your blonde was a loud one, eh?" Robby smacked Levi's arm.

"Not quite *that* way. She screamed when she saw a mouse, which turned out to be a cat toy, then again when Rhi fell out of bed."

"No wonder you're taking her out to breakfast." Robby struggled to unlock his door.

Levi took the keys, unlocked the door, and opened it for his friend. "Get some sleep, man. You look like you need it."

"Party at your place tonight, right?" Robby stumbled into his apartment.

"Right." Levi dropped Robby's keys on the table by the door, locked the handle from the inside, and closed it.

"We'll grab some greasy truck stop food for him on the way back." Rhi linked her arm with Levi's as they strolled down the hall.

"*We* could get greasy truck stop food instead of going to Bellerose." He smiled as he pressed the button to call the elevator.

"But they don't have mimosas, and the steak and eggs taste so much better at Bellerose."

Levi kissed her forehead. "You're right."

Rhi rested her head on her best friend's shoulder. "You're driving, so I'm drinking at *least* two mimosas because of my early morning wake-up."

He chuckled as the elevator doors opened. "Deal."

Chapter Two

Levi

amn, she's hot in that dress.

Levi pulled out Rhi's seat before taking his own.

The waitress sashayed over to them and flashed a smile his way.

She must be new. Haven't seen her before.

"Hi, I'm Alice. What can I get you two?"

"She wants a mimosa. Better make it two. Been a rough morning for her." Levi winked and sat back in his chair, not bothering to hide that he was checking her out. *Nice rack, Alice. I'd take you home if Rhi didn't make Bellerose off limits.*

Rhi caught him staring and narrowed her gaze at him. "Sounds about right. And we both want steak and eggs. Steak rare, eggs over easy, super crispy hash browns on the side. And he's driving, so make his a virgin."

The waitress blinked a few times. "Isn't that just orange juice?"

"Well, aren't you just perfect? Leave your number on a napkin. He'll give you a call tonight." Rhi winked.

Alice looked back and forth between the two of them and raised her brows before stopping on Levi. "What did you want to eat?"

"She ordered for me too. We want the same thing."

"Oh, you're dating?" She frowned then quickly forced a smile. "I guess you've been together long enough to know what the other wants. That's so sweet."

Rhi leaned forward and rested her elbows on the table. "Nope, not so sweet. Yesterday was our anniversary and he forgot all about it."

"Naughty, naughty." The waitress shook her finger at him.

Levi folded his arms over his chest and tried to stop a smile from spreading across his face. "Which anniversary did I forget? The first time we met? Our first class together? When we moved in together?"

Rhi put her hands over her mouth. "I can't believe you forgot the first time we made...we made..." Her eyes sparkled and she bit her knuckle.

The waitress's eyes widened as she took a step away from the table. "Can I get you two anything else?"

"Yesterday was the anniversary of the first time we made kinetic sand together." Rhi stifled her laughter.

Levi laughed. "Come on. That was, like, kindergarten. Plus, you're the one who's good with dates."

"I'm going to put this order in." The waitress turned on her heels and shuffled to the back.

"She's new." Rhi sat back and draped her napkin across her lap.

"Probably not coming back now either." Levi snorted. "You're an ass."

"What? We have a no flirting policy at this restaurant, which you were clearly considering breaking."

Levi opened his mouth to argue but snapped it closed. He knew she saw him. "I didn't flirt…nor did I ask for her number."

"You don't ask for numbers. You just take them home."

Max, one of their regular waiters, strolled over to their table, carrying their drinks and a basket of biscuits. "What did you say to the new girl? She's all kinds of weirded out."

"Rhi confused the poor thing from the get-go. Invited the waitress to give me her number then made it sound like Rhi and I are sleeping together. I'd say we'll behave next time, but that's highly doubtful." Levi sipped his orange juice.

"No, it all started when *he* broke our no flirting rule." Rhi grinned.

Max rolled his eyes. "I knew better than to send a rookie to deal with you two. I will be out shortly with your meals. Try not to take any eyes out with your claws." He patted Rhi on the shoulder.

"Hey, Max? Can we get an order of scrambled eggs, steak well-done, and hash browns to go?"

Rhi turned up her nose. "Just kill good food, why don't you?"

"It's for Robby, dork. He's a stickler for everything being overcooked, remember?"

Max laughed. "It will be waiting when you two are ready to leave."

Rhi shivered. "Remind me never to have Robby cook for me."

"He can't boil water. I don't think you have to worry much about him cooking anything for you." Levi grabbed a biscuit. "Robby's mom undercooked everything, and he ended up with food poisoning one too many times."

"Proper cooking techniques should be a requirement for becoming a parent." Rhi groaned. "Speaking of parents. Mom wants to know when you're coming for dinner next."

"For your mom's cooking? I love her cooking. When does she want us?" Levi licked his lips.

"Well, there's always Sunday dinner."

"Hell yeah, let's go. Maybe I can convince her to make lasagna." He rubbed his hands together.

"If you want that, we can go to the Italian place downtown." Rhi downed half of her mimosa and sat back in her chair.

"Not as good as your mom's. And why do I get the feeling something's wrong?" Levi reached across the table and squeezed her hand.

"I'm fine. Just half asleep and hungry. It was a long night, and I was so rudely awakened too early." Rhi pulled her hand away and picked at her napkin.

"What happened last night? You left kinda early, so I figured you met someone." Levi slid his chair closer to her.

"I went down the bar and grill two doors down. It wasn't as crowded. Ran into a couple of ex-boyfriends… decided it wasn't the night to try and find anyone new." Rhi polished off the rest of her first mimosa and reached for the second. "I'm thinking my whole lifestyle needs to change if I ever want to find someone."

"Maybe you should get some food in you before you start that one." Levi took the full glass and set it out of her reach.

"Levi, why did you—"

Max appeared with their order and placed it in front of them. He tsked at Levi. "I thought you were the designated driver, mister."

"I am. Can you bring her a regular orange juice?"

Max nodded. "On it." He disappeared and returned with the juice almost as quickly as he'd left. "If you need anything else, just holler."

Rhi sliced into her steak and dipped it in her runny egg yolks. "Cooked to perfection as usual."

"What were you going to ask me?"

She shook her head, swallowed, and wiped her mouth on her napkin. "Nothing."

"Come on. I want to know what it was."

She focused on her food then took a drink of her juice. "Why did you have to kick the girl out so early this morning?"

Levi rubbed the back of his neck. "I know that wasn't it. I told you. She mentioned the 'L-word' right after sex. Right after. I had to get her out of there." He leaned forward and stared into her eyes. "Now, tell me what you wanted to ask me."

Rhi held up her hands. "Freeze."

Damn.

Freeze was their way of stopping a conversation they didn't want to have. If one of them said it, the other immediately halted and changed the subject to something else.

Levi cleared his throat and sat back in his chair. "Which ex-jerks did you run into last night?"

"Kyle and Bryan. Bryan said that I should stop sleeping around because real men don't like girls that do that."

"But it's okay for him to sleep with half the county? Talk about a double standard. I never liked him."

"We dated for two years, and you never said a word."

"You seemed happy. I wasn't going to risk ruining your relationship—or our friendship—to tell you I didn't like the guy. I didn't hang out with you two enough to know he was a true tool until after you broke up."

"Next time I date someone you don't like, tell me. Maybe it'll help me realize he's a tool before the two year mark." She stared at his plate. "Are you going to eat?"

"Right." Levi grabbed his fork and knife and dug into his breakfast.

Ten quiet minutes later, Rhi groaned when she finished her food. "That meal should come with a 'wear loose-fitting clothes' warning."

He slid her full mimosa across the table. "Well, when you wake up from your nap, we can go to the gym to make up for it."

"Who says I'm going to take a nap?" She took a sip of the drink.

"It's eight-thirty on a Saturday morning, you've been awake for two hours, sounds like you had a rough night, and you're working on your second mimosa." Levi tapped the glass. "Not to mention the food baby you're digesting."

Rhi laughed. "I guess you're right." She drained the rest of the mimosa. "Flag Max down and let's get out of here."

MAY 9TH

L evi polished off the last of his beer and watched the brunette woman beside him stand and grab her phone. "Hey, it's still early. I'll buy you another drink."

"I have to work tomorrow and have way too much on my mind to drink anything else."

Levi flashed her a smile and then turned to the bartender. "Get me another and one of whatever she's drinking."

The woman gave him a perplexed look. "I'm good, thanks." She shook her head but sat down again.

"Tell me what's weighing so heavy on a pretty girl like you."

She studied him for a moment then picked up the fresh Cosmo and drained it. "I broke up with my boyfriend of nine years because I found out he was cheating on me."

He gave a low whistle and held out his hand. "I'm Levi. Let me get you a refill."

"Trista." She shook his hand and smiled. "Yeah, no. Two's my hard limit."

"You're turning over a new leaf. You just dumped a prick. Why not live on the wild side for once?" Levi motioned to the bartender for another. "You downed that. You can't tell me you don't need another." He scooted his stool closer to her, slipping his knee between hers.

"You're too attractive for the old 'get a girl drunk, take her home, and have your way with her' routine."

Levi eased back. "Whoa. No. I'm having a party at my place in about an hour. I was going to try and talk you into coming. If you decide to have sex with me later, I'm all for that. But consensual only and after you've sobered up a bit. I don't take advantage of people."

The bartender set another Cosmo in front of Trista.

"Put that on my tab, but I don't think she's drinking it." Levi's phone chimed and he glanced over at it.

RHI:

Strike one. lol

He surveyed the room, but didn't see Rhi anywhere.

LEVI:

You're not even here. What are you talking about?

Trista picked up the glass and took a sip. "What, I call you out and now you're ignoring me?"

"Calling me out would imply that I did that. Which I don't."

RHI:

I have my sources. Striking out with the
pretty girl next to you.

LEVI:

Considering she's still talking to me, I
don't think that counts as a strike. And
aren't you on a date?

"I guess you're not interested in me going back with you and a night of wild sex." She ran her hand over his leg.

Levi put his phone down and turned around. "I'm very much interested in that."

"Who ya texting? Ex-girlfriend you screw when you can't find anyone else?" She raised her eyebrows.

Damn, this woman can flip a mood faster than a chef flips pancakes. "Um—my best friend. She seems to have spies here and thinks I'm striking out with you."

The woman leaned forward and pressed a kiss to his lips. "I guess we should prove her wrong, shouldn't we?"

"Oh, most definitely. Just give me one minute." He ordered an Uber then sent Rhi a quick text.

LEVI:

Bottom of the ninth, one strike, bases
loaded. Home run.

The woman clutched his hand. "Come on, take me to this party."

"You got it." Levi dropped some money on the bar, snaked his arm around her waist, and moved toward the door. He stopped when they stepped into the other room and he caught a glimpse of Rhi sitting with the guy from the gym—Chad or something. *So, she is here.*

Rhi rubbed her temples.

He frowned.

"You okay?" The woman leaned into him.

"Yeah. I'll be right back. I think I see someone I know." He removed his arm and stormed over to Rhi's table.

Chad narrowed his gaze and pointed a finger at Rhi. "Oh no. I'll pay for dinner because you'll owe me something then."

Fucking jerk. Levi growled as he made his way across the room.

"Fuck that." Rhi rose and motioned for the nearby waitress.

"Can I help you, miss?"

"Can I get my food at the bar? This date is over."

"No way." Chad gripped her wrist with one hand and yanked on her hair with the other one. "We're not done yet."

Levi clutched the back of Chad's neck and squeezed. "I suggest you let her go before I throw you out myself."

"Fuck. Let me go!" Chad whined and released his grip.

The waitress put her arm around Rhi and pulled her away.

Levi withdrew his hand and ran it through his hair as he shot a quick glance at Rhi.

Chad spun toward Levi, glowered, and puffed out his chest. "Who the fuck do you think you are?"

"Whoever the fuck I need to be to get you to leave her alone. Or maybe I should take you outside and teach you how to treat women."

"Fuck off." Chad attempted to shove Levi.

Levi jabbed his finger into Chad's chest. "First things

first. Just because you buy a woman dinner doesn't mean she owes you shit. Second, grabbing *any* woman like that is assault. Everyone has boundaries and you need to learn not to cross them."

"Who knew the slut had standards? From what I hear, you're not that great anyway." He barged past Levi, growled, and stormed out the door.

"I'll see if I can get the manager to take his meal off your bill."

"I'll cover it. Don't worry about it." Levi pulled out his wallet, handed the waitress his card, and then glanced over at the table. "Pack hers to-go." He looked over to where he'd left his date and saw her walking toward the door with another guy. "Looks like she found someone else."

Rhi threw her arms around his neck. "Thank you. And I'm sorry about your date. Go after her if you want."

"Nah, I'm heading back to the apartment. I'm hosting that party in an hour, remember?"

"Oh, yeah." She turned to the waitress. "Hey, I'm gonna eat at the bar. Don't worry about making it to go."

"Are you sure? I have an Uber on the way. You can ride with me. It's not like you aren't welcome there. It *is* your place too." Levi smiled. *Come home with me so I can make sure you're safe and Chad doesn't show up to do something stupid.*

"I'll be fine." Rhi pushed up on her toes and pecked his cheek. "I need to calm down and reset a bit before I can handle that many people in the apartment."

Levi pulled out his phone. "I'll text Robby and have him move it to his pla—"

"No." Rhi put her hand on his arm. "I just need a little time alone, okay? I'll call you if I need you."

He nodded and kissed her forehead. "Be safe, and I don't care what time it is… call me."

"I promise." She squeezed his hand and made her way toward the bar.

He dropped some cash on the table as a tip.

The waitress sauntered over to him and handed him his card back. "You're a good guy." She motioned to Rhi. "Did you two date?"

"She's my best friend." Levi's gaze wandered over to where Rhi was sitting. But she was so much more than that. She was his confidant, the one he went to when he had a problem. And she did the same thing to him. She was the first person he thought of in the morning and the one he wanted to make happy.

"Best friend with benefits, right?" The waitress bumped his arm.

Levi laughed. "Nope." *What would it be like to kiss Rhi?* He shook the thought from his head.

She flipped over his receipt and scrawled her number on it. "I'm done here around midnight if you're still looking for a date."

He tucked the piece of paper in his pocket. "Just remember…I'm a bachelor and one-night stand kinda guy."

"You never know when you might meet *the one.*" She giggled and strolled across the room toward the bar.

Levi glanced at Rhi one more time.

She turned and waved to him.

He tipped his head, shoved his hands in his pockets,

and trudged to the door to find his Uber out front. He climbed into the backseat and smiled at the driver.

"Waiting for someone?"

"Nah. She checked out."

The driver nodded and pulled out onto the street. "Seems early for a guy your age to be calling it a night."

"I'm going to a party."

"Nice. Meeting a girl there?"

Levi shrugged and chuckled. "You know, for the first time in a long time, I'm not interested in taking anyone home."

MAY 9TH

Rhi stopped outside their apartment door. Bass bumped through the walls telling her the party was in full swing.

The door flew open, and Robby put the brakes on before barreling into her. "Whoa, Rhi! You're here. I thought you were going out."

"I did. It ended early. I'm going to grab clothes and go to my parents' house."

"No way. You'll be the coolest girl here. Stay so the rest of us have someone to talk to who's not fawning over Levi." Robby snorted. "Don't move. I'll be right back."

Rhi tapped her foot and held her purse in front of her. She didn't want to deal with people tonight. *Fuck it.* She opened the door and wove through the crowd to her bedroom. She padded inside her room, closed the door, and locked it behind her. "Thank God for locks."

It would be easy to block out the party sounds with headphones. She changed into an old grey T-shirt of Levi's and a pair of white shorts with pandas on them then fell onto her bed and pulled a pillow over her head.

"Hey, Rhi? Where'd you go?" Robby's voice carried over the loud music.

So much for not being noticed. She felt around for her phone and then moved the pillow a smidge.

RHI:

I'm in my room vegging for a bit. Let me have some time, okay?

ROBBY:

K

Rhi turned her phone to silent, put it on the nightstand, and completely covered her head again.

"Hey." Levi tapped on her door. "Everything all right?"

Damn it. Why does he have to notice these things? "I'm fine. Enjoy your party."

"Are you sure?" He jiggled the door handle.

"Yes." The bass from the party was too loud to sleep. She grabbed her phone and wireless headphones, opened her music app, and laid down. Four songs later, the mattress sunk behind her.

Levi pulled out one of her earbuds and tucked her under his arm.

"Sometimes, I hate that you have a key. Leave me alone."

"Not a chance. Did something happen after I left the restaurant?"

"Your waitress let me know she gave you her number." And then she *drilled me on your favorite things and how she could get you to be more than a one-night stand guy.* She inched away and rolled over. "This is why neither of us will ever find anything serious. How many girlfriends and boyfriends are going to be okay with you climbing into my bed?"

"Confirmed bachelor." He smiled and brushed a stray hair out of her face. "And if they want to be with you, they're gonna have to deal with me."

Rhi buried her head against his chest. Her stomach rumbled. "I didn't have lunch and only ate half my dinner."

He lifted her chin and scowled. "I'm gonna have to beat him senseless the next time I see him at the gym. You know that, right?"

She groaned. "Hopefully, he'll never be there at the same time I am again."

"We always go together. You don't have to worry about being alone with him."

"Why do guys have to be creepy—even when the woman *plans* to sleep with them?" Rhi cocked her head to the side. "What happened to the party?"

"They all went to Robby's. We mysteriously ran out of alcohol."

She sat up and scooted away from him. "Why do you do this to me?"

"Do what?"

"Make me feel like an ass for ending your party early? Not to mention your date ditching you. Hell, you could be calling the waitress right now if it weren't for me."

"It's not like I can't go over there too. I moved them one apartment down so you could get some rest." He sat up next to her.

"All right, go. I'm fine. The extra sleep will be good for me."

"That would work and all…but I ordered takeout, and I'd hate to make you eat it all yourself." Levi shrugged.

Rhi met his gaze. *He's smiling, the jerk. I want to wipe that smile off his face. A kiss would do it.* Her face heated, and she covered her mouth with her hand. *What the hell am I thinking?* "Wow, I must have had too much to drink at dinner."

"What? Did you even drink anything?" He quirked his brow.

"No…but that's the only reason I'd ever think about kissing you." She rose and paced the room.

Levi grinned and sat at the end of her bed. "I mean, I *am* a good kisser."

Rhi smacked him in the arm. "Now I *do* need some wine. Where did you hide it?"

"I didn't hide anything. Just told them we were all out." He stood and traipsed into the kitchen.

She followed him, jumping when the doorbell rang. She stepped over to answer the door and smiled when she saw the delivery driver.

"Uh, Levi Morris?"

"I'm his roommate."

"All paid for. Enjoy your evening." He nodded once and turned down the hall.

"Thanks." Rhi took the bags, shuffled over to the table, and unloaded the Chinese takeout boxes.

Levi set plates and forks next to the food and sat down across from her. "Now what would be so bad about kissing me?"

"We're best friends. *Only* friends. We don't kiss. That would completely change our friendship." Rhi plucked an egg roll out of the carton and took a bite. "Plus, you're too conceited and probably suck at kissing." *Better make this a joke.*

"You wanna bet?" Levi walked around the table and knelt so he was at eye level with her.

She shoved him away. "Absolutely not, weirdo."

He stumbled back and fell on his butt. "You're in for it now, Rhi Edgerly."

"I'd throw food at you, but this is too good to waste." She popped a piece of sweet and sour chicken in her mouth and smirked at him.

Levi stood and pulled her against him. "Tell me you think I'll be good at kissing or I'm going to prove it to you." He lowered his lips toward hers.

"Levi—" Her whole body hummed. He's my best friend. *I shouldn't want him to kiss me.*

The front door burst open.

"Whoa."

She pushed Levi back. "Freeze."

Levi raked a hand through his hair. "What do you want, Robby?"

Robby held up his hands. "Looks like you two were getting pretty close to kissing there."

Levi folded his arms across his chest. "Whatever. I was trying to convince her to go to the party."

Rhi took a deep breath, her appetite gone. "I'm going to bed."

Chapter Five

Levi

Levi searched the cabinets for something to eat then opened the refrigerator, staring blankly at the near-empty shelves. The only thing in there was the leftover takeout. He frowned and reached for a container.

Rhi breezed through the apartment door. "You're going to insult my mother by eating before we go over there?"

Levi opened his mouth and then closed it, not sure what to say.

Rhi rested her hands on her hips. "Well, don't just stand there. Come help me get the groceries out of the car."

"Don't we order those?" Levi shut the refrigerator and puckered his brow.

"I felt like going to the store." She shrugged then disappeared out into the hallway.

Levi glanced at the clock before following her. "How much did you get?"

Rhi hit the button for the elevator. "Manda and I spent

the morning together. Breakfast, mani/pedi, mall, and lunch. Then I dropped her off and went grocery shopping." She held up her hands to show off her nails.

"Cute." He propped himself against the elevator wall. "Are you sure you still want me to go with you tonight?"

Rhi waved a finger in his face. "How do you think my mother would take you canceling on her? It's been over a year since you've been there."

"I meant after last night." He shoved his hands in his pockets. "If you aren't comfortable with me being there, I can bow out."

"Oh, come on. You think that's going to change our friendship? Clearly, I was upset, and you were trying to get me out of my funk." Rhi laughed as she stepped into the hallway.

"Right." Levi forced a smile as he followed her out of the elevator, opening the front door of the apartment building for her. He grimaced when her back was to him, thinking how he'd spent most of the night doing everything he could to forget their near kiss.

She popped the trunk of her car and turned around. "Come on, slowpoke. Up late with another clingy lady?"

"I slept alone last night."

She reached over and checked his forehead. "No fever. Are you sure you're actually Levi? Or just some incredibly perfect copy?"

"I knew you thought I was perfect." Levi grabbed a handful of bags.

Rhi rolled her eyes. "I said perfect *copy*—not that *you* are perfect." She hoisted the remaining bags out of the car and shut her trunk.

"I mean, what's not to like? Great body, good in bed, I carry groceries, and I'm never clingy."

"And if you look up the definition of 'modesty,' your picture will be right next to it." Rhi laughed. "Of course, the caption will be, 'the above picture is the opposite of modesty.'"

"But you're not denying the rest."

"Well, you *are* carrying groceries." She opened the door to the building and held it for him.

"I'm *not* clingy."

"Maybe to your one-night stands. But did you eat at all today?" She pushed the elevator button and waited for it to open.

"Ten minutes ago, you yelled at me for trying to eat one of the few things we have in the fridge. I can't eat and carry all of this." Levi grinned as they stepped in. He stared at her across the elevator. Her lips beckoned to him. He wanted to drop the groceries, cup her neck, and kiss her until she admitted he was good at it.

"Why are you staring at me like that?" She inched closer to the elevator door as it opened then hustled to the apartment door.

He followed and kicked the door closed behind him. "I still think you'd think I'd be a good kisser."

She put the bags down and planted her fists on her hips. "You are dangerously close to breaking the freeze rule...and all because of your ego!"

"No way is this all about my ego. I'm just saying I know I'm a good kisser."

Rhi sighed. "I'm sure you're great, Levi. But it's kind of weird thinking about kissing my best friend."

"Weird? Why?" He bristled but inched closer to her. "You're telling me you were creeped out last night?"

"No! I mean. It was different...but not creepy." She glided away from him, bumping into the counter.

Levi stared at her lips. His phone chimed from his pocket. He shook his head and took a step back. *Damn. This is about to go way too far.* "Now who's breaking freeze rules?"

Rhi smacked his arm. "You and your bruised ego started it." She grabbed a grocery bag and emptied it onto the counter.

He forced a chuckle and opened the refrigerator to put a package of cheese away. "Damn ego gets me every time."

"Don't you dare just throw that in there like you always do." She snatched the package and slid it into the bottom drawer. "Cheese is best kept in the vegetable crisper and farthest away from the freezer."

Levi shook his head and pulled his phone out of his pocket. "I'm going to let you finish the groceries."

"Put the veggies in the crisper." She turned back to the mountain of bags.

"That's the one with the cheese, right?" He read the text message from her mother.

JEN:

So glad you're coming to see us tonight.
It's been too long. Bring your appetite. I'm
making lasagna.

Rhi waved him away. "Go get ready to leave. We're heading to Mom's in twenty minutes."

"She just texted me to say she's making lasagna. She must miss me." Levi laughed.

"Well, Mason's home from school."

"Mason doesn't even like lasagna. She's making it 'cause I'm going to be there."

Rhi rolled her eyes. "Nice try. It's one of his favorite foods."

"But not his *favorite* favorite. It's mine though. And your mom knows that."

"If the meal comes with all your favorites, you might be right. If not, she just needed something that would feed a lot of people."

Levi smiled. "I'm going to change."

The front door opened the moment she climbed out of the car. "Aunt Rhi!"

She knelt and opened her arms for her almost six-year-old nephew, Milo.

He jumped and threw his arms around her neck.

"Hiya, buddy, I didn't know you guys were coming home." She hugged him then stood.

Milo beamed. "We're visiting Grandma and Grandpa."

They walked over to where Levi was standing. "Do you remember Levi? He hasn't been here in a long time."

Milo squinted at him, nodded, and waved. "Hi, Levi."

"Hey, bud." Levi reached over and ruffled his hair. "You got bigger since the last time I saw you."

"I'm in kindergarten." Milo beamed.

Levi chuckled. "Are you doing good in school?"

"Yup! Mom and I are going back to Minnesota tomorrow so I can go back to school." Milo ran back to the house and flung open the front door.

Rhi's mother appeared in the doorway. "Are you coming in, or are you standing in the yard all evening?"

"Levi's scared he might get caught with some weird disease like relationshipitis or more-than-one-night-together if he gets too close to anyone who's married," her older brother, Edge, called from behind her.

Levi shuddered. "Those sound awful. Maybe I should stay out here."

"Levi Morris," Jen planted her hands on her hips, "if you don't get over here right now and give me a hug, I will put you over my knee."

Levi leaned over to Rhi. "You and your mom look surprisingly alike in that pose."

Rhi glared at him as they walked toward the house. "I think I'm going to be absent the next time you have a girl over."

"Who's going to kick them out for me then?"

Levi put his arm around Jen. "Hi, Mom."

She squeezed him tight. "It's been way too long since you've been here. No more breaks. You need to be here every Sunday with the rest of the family."

"Yes, ma'am. I'll do my best."

Jen hugged her daughter and motioned them into the house. "Come in, come in. I made all your favorites, Levi."

"Salted caramel brownies?" Levi licked his lips.

"Sure did." Jen nodded.

He glanced over at Rhi. "Told you."

She pinched the bridge of her nose. "Stop stroking his ego. It's big enough."

"Come on. He hasn't been here for at least a year. Of course I went all out." Jen laughed and headed back to the kitchen.

Levi nodded to Rhi's brother and sister-in-law on the couch. "Edge, Sara, nice to see you."

"Don't get too close. Marriage is contagious." Edge chuckled and stood.

"Damn. Guess I shouldn't have hugged your mom."

Rhi hugged her brother. "How long are you all here?"

"Sara and Milo are going home tomorrow. They'll be back when he finishes school. I'll be here until I finish getting the house ready to be sold."

"You're selling it?" She frowned.

He nodded. "Yup."

"But that means there's no chance that you're moving back here."

"Nope, we're happy where we are. Minnesota is a lot more liberal than Indiana. We both love our jobs, and Milo's doing great in school."

She sighed. "I miss my big brother."

"Miss you too."

"Levi." Leon Edgerly appeared in the hallway. "Good to see you. Come back to my office. I have some software I want you to look over."

"Sure." Levi disappeared into the back of the house with her dad.

Rhi considered following her mom into the kitchen, but there was no way she could tell her what she was thinking.

Sara stood up and took her hand. "You look like you need an ear to bend. Let's go to the back porch." She dragged Rhi outside, and they sat down on the wicker chairs looking out across the backyard. "How's the dating scene going?"

Rhi rubbed her temples. "Terrible. The guy I went out with last night was a total creep. Tried to demand he pay for dinner so I would 'owe' him something."

"What a jerk! Is Levi going to pound him for you?"

"Thankfully, he was at the same place and dealt with him right away. I sometimes wonder what I'd do without him. It's dangerous out there." Rhi ran a hand through her hair. "Being a modern, empowered woman sucks. Just because I like to have sex doesn't mean I'm going to sleep with everyone I go out with."

"Unfortunately, people talk. Some will assume you're more…open…than you are." Sara patted her shoulder. "At least you were able to get out of there without any physical injuries." She shuddered.

"I ate part of my dinner at the bar. The waitress talked my ear off trying to pump me for information about Levi." Rhi exhaled. "I ended up going to work for a while then came home and interrupted a party. Tried to sneak in and avoid everyone, but that didn't happen. Levi moved the crowd over to Robby's, ordered Chinese food, and made me talk to him."

"That's sweet. Not many guys would do that."

Rhi focused on her hands. "He almost kissed me last night."

"I've seen him kiss you a lot over the years. That's not surprising at all."

"I meant on the lips. I had this momentary lapse where I imagined kissing him and made a joke about it. It continued for a bit until we were in the kitchen. He held me against him and lowered his head to kiss me."

"Why didn't you let him?"

"Robby came in and interrupted us." Rhi picked at a nonexistent piece of lint on her pants. "I freaked out. Called freeze and went to bed. Not that I slept. I laid awake the entire night thinking about what his kiss could have been like."

"Have you talked to him about it today?"

"No. I left early this morning and spent the day with Manda until it was time to come here. I thought it was going to happen while we were putting away groceries, but he stopped and we joked about it again."

"Why don't you talk to him? Or get it out of your system and just kiss him?"

"I don't want to ruin our friendship. What if it's awkward or gross? Or even worse, what if it's amazing? He's never going to give up the bachelor lifestyle, and I wouldn't ask him to."

Sara rested her elbows on her knees. "What did you just tell me about being a modern empowered woman?"

"That just because I like sex doesn't mean I'm going to have it with everyone."

"But what you're referring to is the reputation that follows you around. Shouldn't it be the same way with Levi?"

"You're right." Rhi blew out a breath. "I don't want to screw up our friendship."

Sara smiled. "I get that. Your brother and I were in a similar boat when we got together. We'd known each other since diapers. The two of us and Jason were inseparable. I was worried when we got together that it would ruin our friendship, but it strengthened it instead."

"How did it do that?"

"We recognized the little things we did for and with each other as showing how much we loved the other."

"I mean, Levi and I do love each other, but it's just as friends."

Sara put her hand on Rhi's shoulder. "There's nothing wrong with the two of you staying friends."

Rhi took a deep breath. She knew she couldn't imagine her life without him in it. But did she love him as more than just a friend? "I don't know."

"Take the next week to think about what you'd want in a relationship. Think about the person you want to spend the rest of your life with. Look at the things you do with Levi and the strong friendship you already have. You may find that the two line up better than you think."

Rhi nodded. She opened her mouth to say something, but the back door creaked open.

"Mom said to tell you dinner's ready."

"Well, hi to you too, Lex." Rhi stood and gave her sister a hug.

She patted Rhi on the back and took a quick step away as if hugging her older sister was a burden. "Is it true Levi came with you?"

Rhi smiled. "Yep."

Lex rolled her eyes. "No wonder Kym's putting on makeup. She's always thought he was dreamy."

"He's a little old for Kym." Sara shook her head.

"Can we go eat now? Or are we going to make this whole thing more awkward?" Lex rocked on her heels.

"We'll be in in a minute." Rhi motioned for Lex to go ahead of her then sat back down. "She's a little weird today."

"She finally came out on Friday. She's dreading telling you because she thinks you're going to freak out. We've all told her you're not, but I'm sure she's even more nervous with Levi being here."

Rhi frowned. "I've never freaked out about anything like that. I'm so glad she's ready now. It's not like we all didn't know. Is Chelsea officially her girlfriend?"

"Dad caught them kissing in the living room the other day. I think that's why they admitted it. He didn't say anything when it happened, but she came out that night at dinner."

"How'd dinner go after that?"

"I believe Mom said 'it's about damn time'. Then she asked if someone could pass the potatoes." Sara laughed.

"Have they shared with the rest of the family? Aunt Serena told me at least five times how cute of a couple they'd make."

"She's not wrong. I think they've told her parents too." Sara looked at the door. "We should probably join them so Lex doesn't slink out again."

"After you."

Rhi followed Sara into the house and down the hallway that led to the kitchen.

Kym walked out of her room wearing a tight maroon long-sleeve midriff shirt and a short black A-line skirt. She grinned at Rhi. "Did Levi come?"

"Glad you're excited to see *me*." Rhi hugged her sister. "Yes, he's here."

Kym squealed and rushed toward the dining room, plowing into Levi as he stepped around the corner from their father's office.

He caught her arms to steady her before taking a step back. "I love your mom's lasagna too, but there's no need to be in that much of a hurry."

Kym blushed and brushed her brown curls out of her face. She planted her hand on her slender waist, cocked her hip to one side, and straightened her back. "Hi, Levi." She twirled a piece of hair between her fingers and batted her eyes.

He took two steps back. "Um."

Rhi padded over and bumped arms with him. "See, even the young ones can't help but flirt with you."

Kym's face reddened even further. "Rhi!"

"Your face matches your shirt now." Rhi chuckled.

"Be nice." Levi put his arm around her and peered at Kym. "No offense, but you're a little young for me."

Kym stormed into the dining room.

"Hitting on my little sister?" Edge stood in the doorway.

"No, never. I mean, she's way too young. I may sleep around a lot, but I draw the line at legal." Levi drew a line in the air with his hands.

"I was talking about Rhi." Edge winked before turning and heading into the dining room.

Levi wrapped his arm around Rhi's waist and pulled her close. "Well in that case, Rhi and I have a secret sex room in our apartment."

Rhi smacked him on the arm. "Oh please, your bedroom isn't a secret to anyone. You have a different girl in there every day of the month."

"Y'all sound like you need a therapy session. And I get paid by the hour, so you might want to get in here before I start charging you," Jen called from the other room.

Rhi walked into the dining room and smiled at the scene in front of her. Her family was together again. All eleven of them.

"Sit next to me, Aunt Rhi." He pointed to the empty chair next to him.

"Well, of course. Your grandma wants to sit next to Levi." Rhi plopped down in the seat next to Milo.

Levi sat down between her and her mother. "They left the seat of honor for me."

Leon leaned forward. "Makes it easier for her to smack you in the back of the head."

Levi nodded. "And with Rhi next to me, I'll get it from both sides."

Rhi looked over at Mason. "How's college going? Have you decided what you're going to do with your life yet?"

"Be a bum on Mom and Dad's couch?" He smiled.

"You're more than welcome to. I don't know what I'm going to do with an empty house once the girls are gone."

"What?" Levi pouted at Jen. "How come I didn't get the offer to be a bum on your couch?"

"Because she'd have to buy stock in bed sheets and laundry detergent." Rhi bumped his shoulder.

Jen shuddered. "Not to mention the amount of therapy sessions I'd be giving away to all the girls you'd be sending home."

Levi glanced over at Rhi. "We should try that next time. You can come out dressed like Sigmund Freud and ask them how they feel about their mothers."

Rhi scoffed. "You think I plan my morning routine?

The only constant seems to be me being woken up by some random woman who was *way* too loud."

"Which routine did you use today?" Lex snorted.

"I was out of the apartment early, so none. Yesterday morning, I started with the threesome thing but got annoyed and kicked the girl out."

Chelsea studied Levi. "How ever did you kick her out on your own?"

"Very funny. I slept alone last night."

Everyone at the table turned to stare at Levi, some blinking, some with their mouths open.

Jen reached over and checked Levi's forehead. "Are you sick? Should I have made chicken soup?"

Levi rubbed the back of his neck. "Just wasn't into anyone." He looked at Lex and Chelsea. "Are you two *officially* dating yet or are you still hiding it?"

"You knew?" Lex stared at Levi and then at Rhi. "Both of you?"

Rhi nodded. "We've all been just biding our time waiting for you two to admit it."

"And you're not weirded out or anything?"

"Why would I be? You're my sister and I love you no matter what. And Chelsea's been here so long, she's already another sister to me." Rhi beamed and glanced around the table. Her family could be a handful at times, but they were always there for each other, and their love was strong.

"Just like Levi and Sara, it doesn't matter if they're friends, wives, girlfriends, or boyfriends. When you've been around that long, you're family." Mason nodded.

"I told you no one would be upset about it." Jen

reached over and squeezed Lex's hand. "We all just want you to be happy."

"Thanks, Mom." Lex gave her a small smile.

Levi's stomach growled. "And now it's time to eat. Rhi didn't let me eat *anything* today."

Rhi rolled her eyes. "Because I locked the refrigerator and the cabinets?"

"No. But you didn't leave any groceries in the house either."

"Poor baby...left with nothing but leftover take out." Rhi shook her head.

Lex grinned. "I don't know how you two are ever going to live without each other. You already act like an old married couple."

Rhi laughed. "Minus the whole sex thing."

Levi smirked. "So *exactly* like an old married couple."

Jen smacked him in the arm. "I'll have you know—"

"No, no, no." Levi held up his hands. "I do not need to know about my secondary parents' sex life."

"Ew!" Kym covered her face. "Do you all have to be so embarrassing?"

Leon picked up a bowl of garlic bread. "Time to eat."

MAY 10TH

Levi wandered into their kitchen and put the leftovers in the refrigerator. "You wanna go see a movie? It's still early and I'm not feeling the party scene. It's almost nonexistent on Sundays anyway."

"Only if the theater is in our living room. I ate way too much and am ready to be in pajamas."

"Go change. I'll do the same, grab a couple beers, and meet you on the couch."

"Sounds good." Rhi disappeared into her bedroom.

Levi strolled into his room and changed into pajama pants.

"Make mine chick beer," she hollered as he walked to the kitchen.

"Always do." He grabbed two bottles out of the refrigerator and plopped down sideways on the couch.

Rhi came out and sat down next to him. "Don't we have a shirts rule somewhere?"

"A shirts rule?"

"Levi must always wear a shirt when hanging out with Rhi."

"Negatory. Levi must never be forced to wear a shirt… unless he's leaving the apartment." He stretched his leg out behind her then pulled her into his arms so she was leaning against his bare chest.

She grabbed the remote and flipped through the options on Netflix. "What do you want to watch?"

"I don't know. You pick something."

She sat up and shifted to look at him. "Okay, something is off. You slept alone last night and you're not hogging the remote to watch some crazy action-filled fuck fest."

Levi snorted. "I watch more than that."

Rhi turned off the TV. "Come on." She reached out and took his hand. "Talk to me. You don't ever hide things from me."

"After you went to bed, I had no desire to go back to the party, so I turned in. No biggie."

"And tonight? You leaving to go out after this movie?"

He shook his head. "After that big of a meal, I'll be lucky if I don't fall asleep on the couch with you."

"What did you and Dad talk about before dinner?"

Levi took a deep breath. "Software stuff and a possible job opportunity."

"What? Working for my dad?"

"Sort of. I guess Mason is more into the sales side of the company. He doesn't want to be behind a desk. He'd rather manage sales, install, and repair."

"The stuff Larry does right now."

"Right. He asked if I would be interested in taking over the software development side someday."

"That's awesome. You could own part of the company and not have to work for anyone else."

"It would also mean moving back to Bryton."

"That's not such a bad thing, is it?" She smiled at him and leaned over to give him a hug. "This is amazing news. I'm proud of you."

Levi paused. "I know your trust fund doesn't mature until next year, so if you need help affording this place when I move out, I can do that."

Rhi sat up. "You think you're leaving me in Indy and moving home alone?"

He let out a breath he didn't know he was holding. "What about your job though? You shouldn't have to give that up to move back with me."

"I can telecommute until I find something closer. It's not like social media can't be run anywhere as long as I have access to the internet."

Levi stared at her before he pulled her back against him, kissing the top of her head. "You're the best." His head spun. *She's willing to drop everything, search for another job, and go back to Bryton without a second thought. Do best friends do that for each other?*

He slid lower on the couch, and she snuggled in close. Heat radiated from her hand the moment she placed it on his thigh. He rubbed his fingers along the silky skin of her arm. *Why have I never noticed how soft her skin is?*

She sat up and moved near the other armrest. "Been a couple days, eh?" Her face reddened, and she folded her legs under her.

"For what?" The words were out of his mouth before he realized how hard he was. "Shit." He snatched the blanket off the back of the couch and pulled it over his body. "Sorry."

"There's no reason to be sorry." She grinned. "It happens, and last time I checked, I wasn't a bad looking girl."

"You're hot, Rhi. Don't let anyone tell you you're not." Levi shifted in his spot. "I think I need to grab a cold shower."

"You don't have to hang out and keep me company. Go pick someone up. I'll think of a new way to kick her out in the morning."

You're the only one I want to pick up and I wouldn't be kicking you out in the morning. He shook his head. "Whoa."

"What? Did you like that idea?" She laughed.

"No. Not feeling it." He blew out a deep breath. "I'm going to..." He let the words trail off, turned, and hurried to his room.

Chapter Eight

Rhi

Rhi sat at the kitchen table, swiping through the matches on her dating app. It had been almost a week since their almost kiss, and everything seemed to be back to normal—for him, at least. She'd barely slept. *I wouldn't even go out if he'd just admit he was interested in me. I'd rather stay in with him anyway.*

Levi took the seat next to her. "Anything good?"

She inhaled the scent of his cologne and smiled. "If by 'good' you mean good material for a comedy, yeah. I'm killing time before the concert." She handed Levi her phone. How could she get her profile to end up on his account? She knew everything about him, and they had the same interests, so it was weird he hadn't shown up on hers. "How about you?"

Levi shook his head and passed his phone over to her. "I think I've swiped by everyone on the app."

Rhi scanned through his matches. "Oh, here's one. 'You want a bad girl. I'm bad at everything.'"

"Ha." He held her phone up and shrugged. "He's a kindergarten teacher."

"I don't like kids enough to be with a teacher." She looked closer at the profile. "It also says he's a coach, but they require him to teach to get paid."

"Fucking assclown. Who writes that on a profile and doesn't get fired?" Levi cringed.

"Evidently this guy." Rhi sneered and peered back at Levi's phone. "This one put a cat filter over her face and is pretending she's a cat."

Levi shook his head. "Nah. Not into the furry thing. How about the guy dressed like a unicorn?"

"No way! And wasn't that a fake profile?" She looked at her phone and let out a breath. No to unicorn guy. "She's cute. Oh wait. She's in Jamaica. Whoops." She scanned through more profiles then clicked the button to see if anyone was in his saved history. She smiled when she saw her own profile. Maybe something was there after all.

"What?" He glanced over her shoulder.

She swiped on the screen before he could see her profile. "Another furry funny."

Levi handed her the phone back. "Guess it's the bar then."

"Concert with Megan, remember? You're on your own." She loved going to concerts but wished Levi was going with her instead of Megan. They were friends but he made things fun.

"Oh, right. I should scalp a ticket somewhere and go with you two."

Rhi tapped her fingers on the arm of the couch. "Megan will just get drunk and hang all over you. You know she's wanted you for years."

"Not interested in the slightest. She's a nice girl and all, but being your friend makes it awkward." Levi shook his head.

She continued to swipe through his matches. "Wait, here's one. She's a wannabe reality TV star."

"Nice." Levi grabbed his phone and read the bio. "She's cute and sounds like she might be into a one-night stand."

"Perfect for you." She tossed her phone on the coffee table. *Guess it's back to business as usual. More one-time dates and one-night stands.*

Levi sent the lady a quick message. "If all goes well, we both have plans tonight."

"Have fun with your reality star." She didn't want to talk about his date. She sprung to her feet.

"Probably not as much fun as you'll have with all the guys at your concert." Levi stood and wrapped his arms around her.

She pushed against his chest. "You wish. I'll come home shouting because my ears are blown. And I'll be surprised if I don't have a contact high."

Levi laughed and pulled her in for a quick hug. "Please don't let anyone take advantage of you. Call me if you need me?"

"Why, Levi Morris, if I didn't know any better, I'd say you cared." She smiled as her body warmed.

"Maybe." He shrugged. "Now go get dressed. Wouldn't want to make Megan wait."

Rhi darted to her room. *What if he comes home with the reality star? Could I kick her out in the morning without acting like a jealous bitch?* She picked the dress up off her bed. *Nothing changed. We're not dating. It wasn't even a kiss...*

Just...
Almost.

MAY 15TH

L evi yawned as he waited for his date. *Why am I here? I want to be with Rhi, not with some random wannabe reality star.* He glanced at his watch and grabbed his phone. It wouldn't take much to scalp a ticket so he could join them.

LEVI:

> Fifteen minutes late. Another ten and I'm meeting you at the concert. I'll risk Megan hanging all over me.

He took a sip of his beer and stared at the door, silently planning his escape.

A woman shimmied in, talking loudly into her phone.

"No, I won't. I'm going on a date." She rolled her eyes and turned to the three people behind her, all carrying a piece of filming equipment. "Remember, anything too bad can be taken out in editing." She pulled off her sunglasses and fur wrap, fluffing her hair as she looked for the hostess. "There you are. I'm here to meet Levi Morris."

Great. Levi sunk down in the booth.

The hostess turned around and quickly spotted him. "He's right this way, miss." She flashed a grin and escorted the woman to Levi's table.

Levi held out his hand. "You must be Stephanie."

"Oh please, call me Stephie. That's what everyone on the show will be calling me." She looked at the three men videotaping everything. "Make sure to edit out that last part. We'll start the introductions over." She smiled back at Levi. "Levi, wonderful to meet you in person." She air-kissed both of his cheeks.

"Great to meet you too, Stephie." He motioned to the seat across from him. "This place is top end. I'm sure you'll enjoy whatever you have."

She gestured to the others and waved a hand in the air. "Please, no promos. I'm not paying anyone one cent of the money I make for this. And believe me, it will be a lot."

"Ohhkay." Levi sat down. "What are you filming?"

"It's a reality television show about myself, of course." She gave a smile for the cameras. "Tell me about yourself?"

"Well, I'm a software developer at a firm downtown." He paused.

"Oh, no, that won't do." She made the cut sign to the cameramen. "You need to be something different. Something spectacular. Like the CEO of your own company. Something no one would believe because you're so young. Right? Nineteen I'd guess?"

"Twenty-four. I'm not the CEO of my own company, and I'm not going to pretend to be anything I'm not, no matter how many cameras are here." Levi shook his head.

"Oh, I see. A rebel without a clue, I see." She gave a

haughty laugh and motioned for the men to roll again. "Such a rebel and so young. How old were you when you first started at your company?"

"I started working there in college and became a full-time employee after I graduated."

"No way you're a college graduate. You're way too young to have graduated already." She rested her head on her hands and batted her eyelashes at him.

Levi's phone chimed. *It better be Rhi ready to save me from this fresh hell.*

"You're *not* going to read a text while you're on a date, are you? That's rather rude."

"Lady, you brought cameras and three men to our date. You're recording me, without my permission, and trying to make me something I'm not. If my phone goes off, I'm going to answer it." Levi grabbed his phone.

> RHI:
>
> Unless you're with the love of your life, I need you and I need you now. My so-called friend locked me out of her apartment and all my stuff is still in there.

"Shit." Levi took out his wallet and dropped some cash next to his empty beer bottle. "Enjoy your show. I gotta go."

"Wait, no way. No one walks out on me."

"I don't do second dates, and I've crawled over better women to go play with myself in the corner. You want a reality show, go do it somewhere else." He tapped his finger on the table. "Unless you got the owner's permission to film in here, this better not end up anywhere he or I will see it. If it does, you'll be talking to a lawyer." Levi vaulted to his feet and hustled out of the restaurant. "I need my car—quick. Rhi's in trouble."

The valet tossed him his keys and pointed to the car. "It's right over there."

"Thanks, man." Levi texted Rhi before he jumped in the car. *She's been friends with Megan for years. Maybe it was a mistake.* The trip took a little over ten minutes, but it felt like an hour. He pulled into the parking lot and saw her sitting on the front steps of the building. He threw the car in park, got out, and ran to her. "Are you okay? What happened?"

MAY 15TH

"I left my stuff at Megan's apartment, like I always do. Only this time, when we got back, she rushed to the door and slammed it before I even got there."

"Did you knock? Try to call?"

Rhi paced back and forth. "Of course. She won't answer the phone or the door. Hell, she had the super escort me down here."

"Fucking bitch. Did you call the cops?"

"She's one of my best friends in Indy. Or was? Do you think I want to call them on her?" Rhi sank onto the concrete steps and buried her head in her hands.

"She made that decision for you when she asked the super to have you removed." Levi pulled out his phone and dialed 911. He relayed the story to dispatch then handed it to Rhi to fill in the details.

A man scurried out of the building and over to them. "I'm going to have to ask you two to leave. We've had some complaints about you two hanging out in the parking lot. If you don't vacate the property now, I'll be forced to call the police."

"No need. They're on the way. One of your tenants has her purse, which includes the keys to her car and our apartment. That's theft." Levi held up his phone. "And you better believe I'm recording this conversation."

"All I know is Megan said this woman was bugging her and wouldn't stop beating on her door. Then she called about the two of you out here."

"Well, she's about to get a rude awakening by the cops." Levi shook his head.

It didn't take long for the officers to arrive, and they headed up to the seventh floor.

Levi stood at Rhi's side, his arm around her. "It will be okay."

"Police." One of the officers knocked on Megan's door. "Open the door."

The door popped open a couple of inches, and Megan peeked through the gap. "Good. You're here." She closed the door and unhooked the chain to open it all the way. "Some lady wouldn't stop beating on my door then hanging out in the parking lot of my building. I'm scared to death."

The officer motioned to Rhi. "Is this the woman?"

Megan threw her hands over her mouth. "OMG! Rhi did you see the woman beating on my door? I was super scared. She even followed us up to my apartment. That's why I slammed my door so quick."

"You have my purse. *I* was banging on your door and calling you to try and get it back. The keys to my car, which is in your parking lot, are in that purse." Rhi pursed her lips. *She's going to play that game?*

"There was seriously someone else out here. I swear." Megan reached inside her apartment and grabbed Rhi's purse. She handed it to her. "Sorry about locking you out. I was seriously scared."

The officer cleared his throat and looked at Rhi. "Do you want to go through your purse and make sure everything's there?"

She quickly scanned the items in her purse and didn't see anything missing. Her keys and wallet were there, which were the most important things. She checked inside her wallet. "It's all here."

"Excuse me." Megan tapped her foot on the ground. "Can I file a complaint about the woman who was chasing me?"

"If you want to. We'll have to look at the surveillance footage. If it turns out to be your friend trying to get her belongings back, it will look like you were planning to steal her stuff."

Megan huffed, bolted back into her apartment, and slammed the door.

"Okaayyy." The officer turned to Rhi. "There will be a report filed about this. It will include both sides that I heard. Is there anything you want to add?"

Rhi shook her head. "I'm just happy to have my things back."

The officer nodded. "Good. If it turns out you're missing anything, reach out in the morning." He pulled out his card and handed it to her with a smile. "If you ever find yourself single, my cell number's on there too."

She smiled. "I am single. Levi's my best friend."

"Well, then the name's Brant." He extended his hand to her. "Give me a call sometime. We'll go out."

"I'll do that." She shook his hand then turned to Levi. "Ready to go?"

"More than ready." He followed Rhi out of the building and scowled.

"What's up with the face?" Rhi bumped his shoulder. *Is he jealous?* She held onto her purse like it was a lifesaver.

Levi put his arm around her. "What if we'd been dating and the guy asked you out? How rude is that?"

"I mean, we're not, so it's not an issue. But yeah, I'd agree it would be rude if we were. Maybe he could tell we're just friends."

"He said 'if you find yourself single.' He was going to give you his number whether you were dating me or not. Sounds like an arrogant prick."

"Well, if it makes you feel better, the only reason I would call him is if I end up missing something." Rhi kissed his cheek. "Do I detect a hint of jealousy?"

"No! Just because you got everything back doesn't mean you weren't robbed. Of course I'm going to be protective of you." He pulled her into his arms and held her close. "Next time you go to a concert, take me with you."

"Next time, I'll leave my stuff locked in my trunk and I won't be going with Megan." She blew out a breath. "I'm going to go home. Feel free to go back to your date."

"Nah. I'm following you." He snatched her keys, unlocked her car, and checked for anything out of the ordinary. "Looks safe, but if there are any problems, stop and we'll call the garage."

She gave him a fake salute. "Yessir."

He waited for her to climb in and start the engine before returning to his vehicle to follow her home.

Levi was yawning when they made it back to their apartment.

Rhi hugged him after she closed the door. "I hope I didn't ruin a great date, but I will always be thankful you were there for me tonight."

"It wasn't going anywhere. And I wouldn't want to be anywhere else."

"I couldn't believe she'd do that to me. I've known her almost as long as I've known you." She pulled her long hair up into a loose bun. "I'm scared. What if she tries to steal my identity? All my identification and cards were in my purse. I don't even know what to think."

"Call your dad in the morning. Doesn't part of his company handle identity theft issues?"

"Uncle Cory does some of that." She yawned. "I'm not exactly sure what, but they'd know what I'd need to do."

"At least there's a police report out there, so if anything does come up, they should be able to trace it back to her."

"We can hope." Her hands trembled. "You up for sleeping in a comfortable bed with a woman who's not your type?"

"Always. But where will you sleep?" He winked at her. "Let me go change and I'll meet you in your room."

Rhi smacked his arm. "Thank you."

"Anytime, babe. Anytime." Levi changed into a pair of

black pajama pants and a white T-shirt, grabbed a couple waters from the fridge, and headed to Rhi's room.

She was leaning against her headboard, her hands covering her face. "I don't know what bothers me more… the fact that she could be stealing my identity right now or that she was my friend."

"You caught this early and should be able to get everything squared away. Losing the friendship is going to take a lot longer to get through."

"It hurts more than I care to admit." Rhi wiped away her tears and stretched out on the bed.

Levi pulled back the covers, laid down, and drew her against him. "I can't offer you words of wisdom, but I can be your ear and your comfort."

Rhi turned over and kissed his cheek. "Don't ever leave me, Levi. I don't think I could stand it."

"You can't get rid of me that easily. Who's gonna do my laundry or make sure I eat?"

She laughed. "You're an ass, but I love you."

"You better believe it, love."

Chapter Eleven

Rhi

Rhi changed into her little black dress and looked in the mirror. *Perfect.* After a quick fix of her messy bun, she slipped into her black flats and made her way into the kitchen. *Two can play that game. If Levi's still going to meet other women, I'll be going out too.*

Levi stared into the fridge then walked over to the counter, his jeans and white tee snug on his frame. "Hot date? I thought you were going to change your whole lifestyle when it came to dating?"

"I am. I let Robby set me up with a friend of his."

Levi frowned. "That doesn't sound promising. You guys have nothing in common."

"I guess this guy's a fellow cat lover. Robby said he has quite a few."

"So, a crazy cat guy? Forty and living in his mother's basement, right?"

Rhi crossed her arms. "He's our age, his name is Jerry, and he owns his house."

"Jerry? Who names a kid our age Jerry?"

"Well, his mom, of course." She grinned as Duke jumped up on the island and strolled closer to her. She reached out and petted the cat. "Maybe Mommy will bring a friend home for you?"

Duke nuzzled her hand before he bit her finger.

"Ouch."

Levi chuckled. "I don't think he wants a friend."

"I bet he'd like a female friend."

"He's fixed, remember? No kittens out of him." Levi walked over, and Duke hopped onto his shoulder. He scratched him under the chin, and Duke purred. "Just a couple of grumpy bachelors, aren't we, Duke?"

Rhi rolled her eyes. "Grumpy because neither of you are getting laid tonight?"

"Nah. My date will be here in about ten minutes. So get lost before then, will you?"

"Lucky for you, this friend of Robby's knows we live together."

"And he's cool with it?" Levi leaned against the counter and folded his arms.

There was a knock on the door.

"Yup! He think's your gay." Rhi winked and opened the door.

"Rhi?" Jerry handed her a half-shredded bouquet.

"Thank you." She forced a smile.

He looked a lot older than twenty-three. His forehead was wrinkled, and more gray hair was on his head than brown. Deep laugh lines appeared when he smiled. "Sorry. My cat got into them. I figured you'd understand." He shifted from one foot to the other.

"I do." She took the flowers and walked over to the counter.

"Oh, honey, let me take those. You don't have a lick of fashion sense at all." Levi grabbed the bouquet and reached for a vase. He leaned close to Rhi and whispered, "Our age, huh?"

She smacked his arm. "What do flowers have to do with fashion sense? And I thought I looked good in this."

"Well, duh, you do. But then again, I picked the damn thing out." Levi turned around and waved his hand in the air. "You should have seen the ugly thing she was wearing before you came in. Practically a burlap sack. It was hideous and said 'old grandma who's going to be a cat lady for the rest of her life.'"

Jerry smiled. "I love cats, so I'm down for that."

"Oh, honey, are you just as hopeless as she is?" Levi put his hand on Jerry's shoulder. "Just take her out and have a good time. I'll be leaving soon. I won't wait up." He threw the flowers in the vase and sashayed to his room.

Rhi burst out laughing. "My roommate is crazy. Don't mind him."

"It's all right. Are you ready to go? I have the cat in the car." He motioned to the door with his thumb.

"You brought a cat?" She darted to the door. "It's like eighty outside. Are we dropping him off before we go out?"

He followed her out into the hallway. "Yeah, sure. Robby said you were into cats, so I figured I'd let you meet him."

"Ohhkay." Rhi nodded.

She opened the door to the stairwell, and they sped down and out to the parking lot.

Jerry fumbled with his keys and unlocked the ancient Buick. He leaned into the backseat to check on the animal.

Rhi sat in the passenger's seat and spotted the most overweight cat she'd ever seen. "Do you have any water in here?"

The poor ginger and white thing panted then released a meow-like bellow.

"I think so. Let me check." Jerry popped the trunk and hurried to the back of the car.

She reached back and petted the cat's head. "It's all right."

Jerry came back with the water, and his hands twitched when he opened it, dumping half the bottle all over the front of Rhi's dress. "I'm sorry." He poured what was left into a small container in front of the cat.

Rhi stared down at her wet dress. Urgh. *At least it's black and will dry quickly.* "What's his name?" She glanced in the back again.

The cat moved its paws toward the bowl but kept most of its rear end on the seat.

"Pumpkin," Jerry sat again and put his seatbelt on. "Ready to go?"

"Yeah, we are dropping him off, right?"

"Oh, I figured we'd hang out at my house. It's a great place for cat lovers." He flashed her a smile, started the car, and turned the air on high.

Rhi shivered as the cold breeze hit the wet part of her

dress. Wonderful. "Besides being a cat lover, tell me about yourself?" She ran her hands up and down her arms as goosebumps formed.

"There's not a lot to tell. I live in my mother's basement. Well, technically, it's mine. I own the house. And she pays me to take care of all her cats."

"Wait. You own the house, but you live in the basement? Isn't there a room upstairs you can use?"

"Well there is, but where would the cats sleep?" Jerry laughed.

Rhi opened her mouth to respond, but the most horrific sound came from behind her.

Pumpkin let out a half yowl, half wretch as he lost the contents of his stomach all over the backseat.

Rhi cringed, and her eyes went wide. "Ohmigod, we have to stop now."

Jerry shot a look in the back. "Oh, shit." He pulled into a nearby gas station.

She jumped out of the car and ran inside. She scanned the store until she saw paper towels and rushed to get them. Her shoe connected with something slippery and flew out from under her. She landed square on her ass in whatever she'd just slipped on.

"Are you all right, ma'am?" The young man from behind the counter tried to keep from laughing, but his eyes showed mirth.

"Peachy." She got to her feet and looked down at the mess on the floor. "Someone should clean up the cheese sauce. Although, I think most of it's on my dress." She inhaled slowly, marched over to where the paper towels were, grabbed the roll, and stormed back to the counter.

The clerk chuckled and shook his head. "Seriously, they're on me."

"Thanks." Rhi snatched the towels and hurried out of the store to the car.

Jerry sat in the front seat, cuddling his dry heaving cat.

She ripped open the package and opened the back door. The smell hit her immediately. "Oh, God." She covered her nose and backed away. "I'm not sure I can clean that up."

"Don't worry about it." Jerry waved his hand at her. "She does it every time we go to the vet too. I'll have it detailed tomorrow."

Pumpkin stepped over to the passenger's side and sniffed at her, letting out a soft meow.

"I'm not going to be able to get back in the car." The paper towels fell from her hand, and she bent over to pick them up. She was in the process of standing when she felt something touching her butt. She spun around and jumped back. "W-was your cat just licking the cheese off my dress? I'm just gonna have my roommate pick me up."

"That's probably best. I'll be watching Pumpkin pretty closely tonight." Jerry gave her a crooked smile. "Give me a call tomorrow and I'll come get you without the cat in the car. We can hang out and play on the human and cat tower I made."

"Um, I'll think about it." Rhi shut the passenger's side door, pulled her phone out of her purse, and stepped onto the sidewalk. She texted Levi first.

RHI:

When you get done with your date, can you come get me? I'm like a mile from home at the gas station.

Her next message was to Robby.

RHI:

Seriously? You set me up with a guy who lives in his mother's basement and takes care of her cats for a living?

The kid from behind the counter walked out and lit a cigarette. "You sure you're okay?"

"I'm fine. I called a friend to come and get me."

He looked her up and down. "I could take you home after my shift. I get off in an hour."

"My roommate will be here faster."

"Cool. Well, if you're still here when I'm done, hit me up." He nodded and went back to smoking.

Rhi's phone chimed.

LEVI:

Thank you! I was just about to send you a mayday text. Be there in ten minutes.

RHI:

That bad, that quick, huh?

She tucked her phone in her purse. She shifted her dress to the side to see what was left of the mess before stalking into the bathroom to clean herself up.

Levi pulled up as she walked out of the gas station. He rolled down his window. "Hey, pretty lady. Need a ride?"

"Always. Do you have a towel in your gym bag?"

"Maybe? It might be a little ripe though. You forgot to take it inside last time."

"*I* forgot?" Rhi reached through the window and pressed the trunk button. She grabbed the towel and caught a whiff of it. *Ew.* Hurrying over to the passenger's side, she arranged the towel, sat down, and closed the door. "I guess the smell is better than cheese sauce on your seat."

"Do I want to know?"

"The cat was in the car. He threw up. Jerry spilled water on me, and when I was trying to get paper towels from the gas station, I slipped and fell in a puddle of cheese sauce. But *please* tell me how much *worse* your date was."

Levi scoffed and pulled onto the road. "She was naming our babies before we left the apartment. Said she wanted to name the kid Bentley and call him Bentie for short. Not Bennie, Ben, Bent, or even Lee. Bentie."

Rhi chuckled. "Okay, not quite as horrific as mine but still bad for you. Why do we do this?"

"You ask me that every time you have a bad date, Rhi. And I tell you the same thing. We have needs."

"If it was just for sex, I'd get Bob out and call it a day. I have yet to meet a man who'd be worth keeping around just for the sex." She rested her head against the leather seat. "I want someone I can live with for the rest of my life. Be happy and be me."

Levi flashed a grin as he pulled into the parking lot of their building. "Then keep living with me."

Rhi blew out a breath and glanced over at him. Would that be such a bad idea? He was the one person she didn't have to pretend to be someone else around. He'd seen her at her worst and was still there. She kissed his cheek. "You know I love you, right?"

"Yep." He kissed her forehead. "Now go change into sweats. I'll grab the ice cream, and we can plot your revenge on Robby."

"That sounds like the best idea either of us have had all night."

MAY 17TH

Levi parked in front of the restaurant.

His date, Claire, unbuckled her seatbelt and reached for the door handle.

"Wait, I'll come open it for you." He flashed her a grin.

"Ooo, how *romantic*." She batted her eyelashes at him.

Levi's smile faded. He climbed out of the car, walked around, and opened the door for her.

She pulled the door shut.

He tapped on the window and frowned at her. *Another date from hell? Why do I do this to myself?*

Claire blushed and opened the door herself. "I'm so sorry. I panicked. Not used to anyone opening the door for me."

"I just told you I was going to do that." He cocked his head to the side and held out his hand.

She took it then snatched her hand back, blushing again. She put her hand in his again. "Sorry. I've been up for, like, the last thirty-seven hours."

"Maybe you should go home and get some sleep?" Levi helped her to her feet and shut the door behind her.

She jumped when the door closed. "Just a little on edge. No biggie."

Levi blinked twice then sauntered up to the valet and handed him his keys. "No joyrides this time, Mark." He winked at the man.

"Always one with the jokes, Mr. Morris." The valet smiled. "Your table is ready. I hear the chef has a surprise meal for you."

Claire swooned. "Sounds like you're someone important."

"Just well connected." Levi leaned toward Mark. "This may be an early night. Park it close."

Mark nodded once. "It will be ready when you are."

Levi slipped him a bill, turned back to his date, and offered her his arm. "Shall we?"

Claire swayed on her feet. "What?" She blinked several times in rapid succession, a blank stare on her face.

"Let's go in." He wrapped his arm around her. The last thing he needed was her falling over as they walked inside. If anyone saw them, they might think he drugged her.

She stumbled. "Sure."

He forced a smile as he opened the door, ambling up to the hostess kiosk. "Hey, Mary."

The hostess raised a brow toward Claire then turned back to Levi. "Is she all right?"

"I've been up for thirty-seven hours now." Claire perked up and smiled. "I'm gonna need coffee and another Adderall before I go home with this hunk of man." She poked Levi's arm.

Levi pinched the bridge of his nose. "A pot of coffee would be great."

"Of course." Mary led them to the table, quickly excusing herself.

Claire slid into the booth first and let out a sigh. "Ohmigod, I've never been in a booth this comfortable in my life." She rested her head back against the wall and closed her eyes.

Levi sat beside her, pulled out his phone, and texted Rhi.

LEVI:

Strike one. She's been hopped up on caffeine and Adderall for thirty-seven hours. Strike two. We just sat down and I think she's asleep.

He patted Claire on the hand. "Why don't I take you home so you can get some sleep?"

Her head shot up, and she shook herself awake. "No way. Sorry. I totally zoned out there for a moment." She grabbed her purse, opened a pill bottle, and downed a pill with a whole glass of water. "This will kick in shortly."

"Here's your coffee, ma'am. Do you two know what you want to eat? Or do you need a few minutes?"

Levi smiled at the waitress as she set the coffee pot and mugs on the table. "I heard the chef had a surprise for me."

"He does. He wants to try out a new beef Wellington recipe on you."

"I can't wait." Levi nodded then peered at Claire.

Her eyes were closed, and her head hung at an odd angle.

"Claire?"

She popped up again. "Something with caffeine. Damn. I can't seem to shake this tiredness."

"For dinner, ma'am."

"Right." Claire stared at the menu for so long Levi wondered if she had fallen asleep again. She raised her head and smiled. "How about the portabella burger? I can't eat meat. Total vegetarian. You are too, right?"

The waitress took the menu. "I'll be back with your food."

Levi quirked a brow at his date. "The chef's making me a new beef Wellington recipe. Yeah, not a vegetarian."

"Oh, well, maybe it will be made with mushrooms instead of steak. I can't even watch anyone eat meat. It makes me sick. How can you eat the rotting carcass of an animal?"

Levi ran a hand through his hair. "It's not rotting if it's been processed right." He tapped his phone and checked his texts.

RHI:

Ha. I'm bingeing Outlander on Netflix.
Sam Heughan is hot!

Levi snickered.

LEVI:

Remind me not to come home any time soon.

Claire snored next to him.

LEVI:

This date isn't going to last long. Strike three. She's a vegetarian and hates watching people eat the rotting carcasses of animals.

She opened her eyes and peeked over his shoulder. "Who you texting?"

Levi moved his phone away so she couldn't see then slipped it into his jacket pocket. "My best friend."

"Sure you were." She took a big drink of her coffee. "I'm a college student, by the way. I was working on a huge research paper. That's why I've been up for thirty-seven hours. I'm doing it on the effects of sleeplessness on the brain."

"And your professor encouraged you to take medication and do this research on yourself?"

"I mean, I can't force other people to take drugs and go without sleep, so who better to do it on than myself?" She smiled and took another drink. "This coffee is so good."

"There are probably numerous studies out there already. Why not pool the rest of the research and do a meta-analysis?"

"That sounds like way too much work. Why do that when I can stay up for as long as I can and write what happens to me?"

"You do realize taking drugs and forcing yourself to stay awake with massive amounts of caffeine is dangerous to your health, right? People have died from ingesting too much caffeine." Levi rubbed his temples. As much as he wanted to end this, he couldn't leave her there. What would happen if someone took advantage of her?

"That is so not going to happen. My heart is super healthy. I've been taking care of it my whole life."

"Right." Levi nodded. "You're a vegetarian."

Claire rested her head on the back of the seat and closed her eyes again.

RHI:

Do you need a way out? I could totally come up with an emergency for you.

LEVI:

Just come to Preston's and I'll buy you dinner.

RHI:

You're out and I'm getting a home run. That's not fair to you.

He chuckled.

Claire sat up. "Did you say something?"

"Nah, go back to sleep. I think you need it." Levi flagged down the waitress.

"Do you want your food to go?"

"Rhi's on her way. Can you ask Earl if he can throw another one of those beef Wellingtons together?"

"He was making two anyway. Didn't figure your date would be a vegetarian."

"Neither did I." Levi sighed.

LEVI:

It would only be a home run if one of us is getting laid. So, unless you're willing...

Claire let out a loud snore and bolted up in her chair. "Whoa. Almost blew my whole experiment there."

Levi fought the urge to chuckle. "You almost did."

"Oh! Did I tell you about my experiment? I'm studying what lack of sleep does to people."

"You're not going to like what I'm eating. Are you sure you don't want me to call you a cab and send you back with dinner?"

Claire yawned and stretched. "No, it's all right. I'm awake now."

Levi nodded as she dropped her head against the wall. Maybe he *should* get their food to go. He checked his phone.

RHI:

Not gonna happen. But good food is a home run to me.

LEVI:

With this date, I'll consider eating at all a home run. Hurry up. Watching this girl sleep is boring as hell.

RHI:

I'm almost there. Took an Uber so I could help if you need it.

LEVI:

You're a lifesaver.

RHI:

You pay me with good food.

Levi glanced over at Claire, who was fast asleep again.

The waitress returned and shook her head. "If I didn't know you, I'd say you drugged her."

"She drugged herself, and instead of staying awake, she

seems to be more tired. Rhi should be here soon. I'm thinking takeout would be better."

"Are you sure she doesn't need to go to the hospital?"

Levi reached over to check her pulse.

Claire opened her eyes then immediately closed them. "Thanks. That was great."

"Taking her back to her dorm room sounds like the best option."

"If you need anything, let me know. I'll have Earl throw some extra vegetarian options in for her."

"Sounds good."

LEVI:

Note to self: No more dating college girls.

RHI:

Oh but they're the only ones who fall for
all your lines.

Levi pursed his lips.

"How does this date even work?" Rhi grabbed a chair from the next table over and sat down across from Levi.

"I text you while she sleeps?" Levi shot her a glare. "And I'll have you know, most of the women I bring home are over college age."

"Well, we know you don't pick up geniuses." Rhi grinned. "Is she even alive? Her color looks off."

"I checked her pulse. She opened her eyes for a moment, closed them, and mumbled something about something being great."

"Aw, even when they're asleep, you please them." Rhi chuckled. "Seriously, though, I'm thinking we should call an ambulance."

"I'm thinking we take her back to her dorm and encourage her roommate or RA to call an ambulance. I don't even know if she has ID on her. What happens if she gets to the hospital and no one knows who she is or where she's supposed to be?" Levi looked over at Claire.

"She wasn't carrying a purse when I picked her up. If she does have an ID on her, it's in a pocket. I'm not digging through those."

"Okay, I'll give you that one. Are we taking her back now then?"

"Sheila said she'd throw together some extra food for her and bring our meals out. We can take her back after that."

"We could call her a cab."

"Right. I hate it when you Uber by yourself. There's no telling what creeps are out there. She's half passed out already. No way am I sending her out with some random stranger who may have bad intentions."

Rhi kissed his cheek. "Don't let anyone tell you you're not a sweetheart."

Levi held his hands up. "Don't *ever* tell anyone that. It would ruin my reputation."

Sheila came out with two brown paper bags. "Hi, Rhi. Bailing Levi out again?"

Rhi nodded as she took the food. "As always."

"There's three to-go meals in yours and two in hers."

"Thanks, Sheila." Levi handed her his credit card.

Sheila shook her head. "It's on the house. Earl's orders."

He frowned, pulled cash out of his wallet, and dropped a fifty on the table. "At least take this as your tip. We're going to take her back to the dorms and call an ambulance if no one else will. I'll text Earl and let him know what we think."

Sheila smiled. "You're a good man, Levi."

"I told him that." Rhi rose. "I'll go get your car and meet you outside."

Levi gently shook Claire. "Hey, it's time to go. They came back with our takeout boxes."

Claire rubbed her eyes. "We ate already?"

"Yeah, you said the portabella burger was excellent, so I ordered you another to go."

"Wow. I don't even remember eating. I must have been out of it, huh?" She ran a hand through her hair. "What are we doing now?"

"I figured I'd take you back to your dorm. You look pretty tired."

"I thought we'd go back and hang out at your place." She rested her hand on his arm.

"Listen. I don't take advantage of people, and in your condition, it's never going to happen. Let me take you back to the dorm so you can get some help." Levi stood and offered her his hand.

She opened her mouth but shut it and staggered to her feet. "Maybe it would be the best idea for me to go home."

Levi wrapped his arm around her waist as she struggled to keep her footing. "You should go to the hospital."

"I'm fine. Just tired. It's no big deal."

"Right." He led her through the restaurant and out to the sidewalk.

Rhi climbed out of the driver's seat of his car. "Good

evening, sir. I'm your Uber driver tonight. Are we ready to go?"

"Thank you, ma'am." Levi nodded and opened the back door. He helped Claire get settled then walked around to chat with Rhi. "Good idea. Thanks."

"I've bailed you out of way too many situations."

"Maybe." Levi climbed into the backseat.

Claire's eyes were closed and she was snoring softly.

"She's in Fletcher Hall at IUPUI." Levi buckled his seatbelt and reached over to buckle Claire's as well. She didn't wake up this time and he checked her pulse. "Seems okay. Let's get her home fast so she can get to the hospital."

"Will do." Rhi took off and wove through traffic as she made her way the six blocks to campus.

Levi checked Claire's pulse again. Still steady. He jostled her, but she didn't flinch. "I'm going to have to carry her in."

"I'll deal with the RA and roommate. What number?"

"I'm not sure. I picked her up outside the dorm."

"Fuck." Rhi pulled into the parking lot near Claire's building and hustled across the street.

Levi shook Claire a little harder, and she jolted upright. "I'm awake."

"Good. I was starting to worry. We're at your dorm. I didn't know what room, so our Uber driver went to get your RA."

Claire grabbed the door handle and got out of the car. She tried to stand but fell to her knees.

Levi raced around the car to help her to her feet. "I think you should go to the hospital."

"No need. I'm fine, seriously." She stumbled, and he helped her move across the street.

A woman rushed out of the dorm and talked briefly to Rhi. She scanned the parking lot until her gaze landed on Levi and Claire. "What's wrong with her? You didn't drug her, did you?"

Rhi moved away and pulled out her phone.

Claire shook her head. "I've been up for thirty-seven hours. I'm doing an experiment, remember?" She moved away from Levi and staggered toward the dorm.

Another woman caught her as she fell through the door.

Levi pointed at Claire. "She popped something while we were at dinner. She said it was Adderall, but she hasn't been able to keep her eyes open since. I didn't want her to get lost at the hospital and no one know where she was supposed to go if it was anything serious. Otherwise, I would have called an ambulance myself."

Rhi trotted back over to where they stood. "I called. They're on their way."

The woman's eyes widened. "Thank you for doing that."

"No problem." Levi turned to Rhi. "I'm ready to get out of here."

"Me too." She handed the woman the bag of takeout. "He ordered extra vegetarian food for her to have as well."

The woman raised her eyebrows. "Who are you?"

"The Uber driver." Rhi clutched Levi's arm. "Come on. Let's get out of here. You're still on the clock."

Levi followed her and sat down in the passenger's seat

of his car. "That was the weirdest date I've been on in a long time."

Rhi laughed. "You can't even call that a date. That was a disaster."

"Agreed. Let's go eat dinner and you can torture me with that Outlander show you were watching."

MAY 18TH

Rhi yawned on the ride to the twenty-first floor. Sleep had been damn near impossible. Her mind spun.

The almost kiss.

The conversation with her sister-in-law.

Possibly going back to Bryton.

Megan stealing her purse after the concert.

Levi acting like he wanted to jump her bones.

Could things get any weirder?

The elevator stopped at the nineteenth floor, and her boss stepped on.

"You look like hell. Late night date?" Delilah Price tapped her black patent leather heels on the tile.

"Just a long weekend." *More like a long two weeks.*

"Well, you can always take a personal day or work from home. It's not like you don't have internet and access to social media from your apartment." She smiled.

"Oh, speaking of working from home. What would you think about me telecommuting on a regular basis?"

"Thinking about moving? Where?"

The elevator came to a stop and they both hustled out. Delilah motioned for Rhi to follow.

"Back home. Levi may be taking over part of my dad's company."

Delilah opened the door to her office, shuffled inside, and closed the door behind Rhi. "Did you marry him over the weekend?"

Rhi took the chair across from Delilah's desk. "No, why?"

"I've known my friend Joann for twenty years. We went to grade school and high school together and shared a dorm room in college. When we graduated, we got job offers in different states. Do you know what happened then?" Delilah sat down in her chair and opened her laptop.

"I'm assuming you went to different states."

"Yeah, because we're best friends and not married. I have a roommate here and she is a woman I'd consider one of my best friends. If she had a job opportunity, I wouldn't drop everything and move with her. I'd be happy for her and let her go."

Rhi shook her head. "Levi and I are different. We've been pretty much inseparable since we were in kindergarten. The longest we've been apart was a month and that was pure torture for both of us."

"Why don't you two just get soulmated?" Delilah rolled her eyes.

"Right. We're friends. Nothing more." Rhi forced a smile. *Are Sara and Delilah right? Could I live without Levi? How much would change if we end up with other people?*

"Honey, you two have the weirdest friendship I've ever

seen." Delilah shook her head. "How far away are you going?"

"Just back to Bryton. But I'd prefer not to have an hour plus commute twice a day."

"I don't like it. I'll think about it...but I don't like it. You'd still have some required meetings you'd need to come down for, but if you end up moving, we'll see what we can do."

Rhi smiled. "Thanks, Delilah. I appreciate it."

"You know, Rhi, you and Levi would make a great couple. The only thing you two are lacking is the sexual part of a relationship and I'm sure that wouldn't take too long if you two looked past your friendship."

Rhi took a deep breath. *Why is everyone bringing this up now?* "Thanks. We're just friends though."

"Whatever." Delilah shooed her toward the door. "Go home and get some rest. No rush on any of the projects. Just make sure you're up to par when you are here."

Rhi nodded. "I may try and work a couple hours here." A yawn escaped.

"Go home. That's an order. I may fire you if you don't." Delilah pointed to the door. "Now."

"Yes, ma'am." Rhi smiled and rushed out the door. She wouldn't get any sleep, but she wasn't going to turn down an afternoon off.

MAY 18TH

F*uck it. Time to go home.*

Levi shut his laptop, leaned back in his chair, and looked at the clock. The day has been a complete waste. He sent his boss a quick message, grabbed his stuff, and headed toward the exit.

The elevator door opened, and Robby smiled.

Levi stepped inside and nodded at his friend.

"Hey, man. Going home already?" Robby glanced at his watch. "Lucky."

Levi rubbed his neck and yawned. "Can't focus anymore."

"I'm so tired of my job. I'd quit in a heartbeat if I had somewhere else to go." Robby yawned.

"Between you and me, Rhi's dad asked me if I would be interested in taking over his company."

"Seriously? Do you need a network administrator?" Robby stood a little straighter.

"Maybe. I'm not sure what positions would be available, but if he makes an official offer, I'd be more than happy to see if there's one for you."

"What's Rhi going to do?"

"She's coming with me."

The elevator stopped at the first floor.

"You giving her a job too?" Robby stepped out into the lobby.

Levi followed, shaking his head. "Nah. She's gonna telecommute while she looks for something else."

Robby snorted. "You two should just get married and get it over with."

Levi threw his hands up. "You just told me you'd come with me. How is that any different than Rhi going with me?"

"I'd only move if I had something lined up. She's willing to telecommute or not have a job at all just to go with you. Come on, dude. I saw you two the other night. You were about to get pretty hot and heavy." Robby bumped Levi's arm. "Admit it. You'd do her."

"I'm not going to do her." With Rhi, it would never be just sex. It couldn't be. There was so much more there. What would happen to their friendship if they did go there? Could they go back to just being friends?

Robby laughed. "The look on your face says you're considering it. You two would be perfect for each other. Maybe the rest of us could slow down trying to keep up with you."

"Keep up with me?" Levi frowned. "I didn't know there was a competition."

"We just want to know when you actually have time to sleep. You bring a different girl home every night and kick her out the next morning. Between the nightly bar run to pick them up and taking them back to the apartment, you have to put in some hours."

Levi smiled. "It's not *every* night, despite how much Rhi jokes. It's mostly weekends, and if it does happen during the week, there's no bars. It's just girls I pick up on the way home."

Robby clapped him on the back. "If you two ever do get together, Rhi's going to have to find new and interesting ways to keep you satisfied." He glanced over his shoulder then back at Levi. "Gotta go. Let me know if you're moving."

Levi nodded and traipsed out the front door. *What would it be like to be with someone on a regular basis?* He'd always dreaded running into any girl he'd slept with before. But the thought of Rhi had his head spinning. He yawned as he climbed into his car. *Maybe a couple hours of sleep will help my head.*

Chapter Fifteen

Rhi

Rhi wrapped herself in a blanket and curled up on the couch to watch a home remodeling show on Hulu. She shoved a handful of popcorn in her mouth and grabbed the remote, clicking through until she found the next episode. The couple on TV spent a half hour arguing about paint colors. Time for a different show. The front door opened, and she glanced back to see Levi walk in. "You're home early."

"I could say the same about you."

"Delilah said I looked like shit and sent me home."

"She was wrong about you looking like shit, but going home early is always a plus." He glanced at the popcorn. "Chinese takeout?"

"That sounds so much better than this." Rhi hurried into the kitchen and searched their drawer with takeout menus. "Where'd you order from the other night? It was great."

"New place on Uber Eats." He opened the app on his phone and turned it toward her. "Same as always?"

"Extra crab Rangoon and egg rolls. I started my period

this morning, so I'm craving super fattening food." She shuffled back over to the couch and snuggled into the blanket.

"Gotcha. Fried fattening food with a side order of cheesecake for dessert."

Rhi moaned. "That sounds wonderful." She rested her head on the back of the couch and closed her eyes. "Hey, did you see the new Marvel movie when it was in theaters? I think it's on Netflix now."

"No. I wanted to see it, but the girl I was with that weekend made me sit through some rom-com that was supposed to make me fall *madly* in love with her."

Something cold touched Rhi's cheek, and she jumped.

Levi held up a Pepsi.

"I see how well that worked, considering you're still single. Was the sex at least good?" She took the bottle. *I hope the sex was awful.*

Levi plopped down next to her. "The only thing I remember from that night was that I wanted to see the Marvel movie."

Rhi smirked and snuggled up next to him. "They should make a rom-com about us. We're funny."

"Kinda hard to be a rom-com when there's no romance."

"There's plenty of romance. Think of how many funny dates we could put in there. Like the time I came home with the guy who tripped over everything. Or all our funny routines in the morning when we kick girls out?"

Levi laughed. "Or the time my dad showed up when you were bringing someone home?"

"OMG that was so awkward…your dad out in the hallway while the guy was dry humping my side."

"That was hilarious. We both got in on throwing him out."

"The look on his face when your dad came up behind him and if he wanted to get in on the foursome was priceless."

"We all had a good laugh at that one."

"What about the time my mom gave you the sex talk?" Rhi turned around and folded her leg underneath her.

"Your mother did not give me a sex talk. Your mother walked me through the entire physical process and went through the psychological process as well." Levi shook his head. "The most embarrassing part was having a girl with me, in public, and being twenty-one."

"See? Amusing romance at its finest."

"But that's not romance. Romance is a special dinner. Or getting your girl's favorite foods, watching her favorite movie, and cuddling on the couch."

Rhi quirked her brow. "Are you trying to say you're romancing me?"

"What? No. I mean. It's different between friends and girlfriends, right?" Levi rubbed his neck.

Rhi looked up at him. "Why does it have to be? If you had a steady girlfriend, you'd do the same thing with her as you do with me."

"Do I have to keep reminding you about the confirmed bachelor status?"

"But what happens if you meet the right girl? The one who makes you want to spend the rest of your life with her?"

"The only girl I would be okay spending eternity with is you."

Rhi straightened herself on the couch, her eyes wide. "Do you even realize what you just said?"

"What? We could live together for the rest of our lives like this and never have a problem."

"So we live out the rest of our lives sleeping around and coming home to each other?" She rubbed her forehead. Could she even do that? She wanted to settle down someday. Maybe even have a family of her own.

"I mean, I'm sure sleeping around will get old eventually but us living together won't. Who knows you as well as I do?"

Rhi blew out a breath and nodded. "That's true." She picked up the remote and turned on the movie. "How long until food gets here?" Everything he'd said recently had her spinning in a different direction.

"Almost an hour. They're busy." He put his feet up on the coffee table and pulled her close.

"Did I tell you Megan called me right before you got home?"

"And you answered?"

"I don't know why but yeah. She tried to apologize. Said something about bad acid at the concert, but I didn't see her take anything."

"Is there such a thing as good acid? And it's not easy to see, but she sounded pretty sober when she talked to the police." Levi laid down and pulled her into a spooning position.

"Yeah, Uncle Cory had me get all new cards and signed me up for a credit monitoring service. If she has any of my card numbers, she can't use them. If she tries to sign up for anything, I'll be notified."

"Good. One less thing you have to worry about."

Rhi stared at the television but couldn't say what the movie was about.

Levi ran his fingers up and down her arm.

Heat shot through her body. Why had she never felt this before when he touched her?

His fingers traveled down her hip and thigh then moved them back up again.

She turned over to face him.

He opened one eye. "Kind of hard to watch TV that way, isn't it?"

"Even harder when your eyes are closed." She snickered. "You're half asleep and confusing me with some bimbo you'll sleep with tonight, aren't you?"

Levi laughed. "No one in this world could ever confuse you for a bimbo. Especially me."

Rhi stared at him for a moment, his lips calling her name. Her skin hummed everywhere their bodies touched.

"I have another funny story for our movie. Remember the time you went on a date and the guy's card got declined. You had to call me because you didn't have your wallet."

Rhi blushed. "And you made fun of me and him the entire way there." That night never did get better.

"Right. And of course I get there and announce—"

Rhi planted her lips on his, immediately cutting his words off. She pulled away just as quick.

Levi's hand curled around the back of her neck, and he

tugged her back to him. His lips moved over hers, tracing his tongue over her lower lip.

Rhi's eyes drifted closed. Her tongue danced with his as fire ripped through her body.

Levi rolled on top of her as he deepened the kiss.

Rhi moaned against his lips.

The doorbell rang, bringing their kiss to an abrupt stop.

Levi rolled off her, pushed himself up, then rested his head in his hands. "Uh, can you get that?"

Rhi sat up and nodded. She rose off the couch, scurried to the door, and opened it.

"Delivery for Rhi Edgerly?"

"That's me." She took the bag from him. "Did we tip you?"

"Yes, very well, thank you." The man smiled. "Have a great day."

Rhi shut the door then put the bags on the table. She dropped into her chair.

Levi slid into the seat next to her. "Still think I'm a bad kisser?"

She scanned his face, the humor she expected to see was absent. "No."

"Scale of one to ten?"

"Are you seriously joking right now?"

"Of course. We just kissed after seventeen years of friendship, and if I don't joke with you now, I may do it again."

"You can quit joking now." Rhi gaped at him. She grabbed the carton of crab Rangoon and took one out of the box.

"I'm serious. If I stop joking, I'll be kissing you again." Levi took one from the container. "So on a scale of one to ten, how good?"

Rhi sighed. "Not to stoke your ego, but ten. Maybe not lifetime, but it's one of the best kisses I've had in a long time. How about you? Where do I stack up?"

Levi took a bite of food, chewed it slowly, and waited until he swallowed before giving her a smirk. "You're right on the cusp between ten and eleven."

Rhi rolled her eyes. "Oh, come on. There's no eleven. It's one through ten."

"There's always an eleven. Because there's the best you've had as a ten and the eleven then becomes better than the best." Levi chuckled.

"Okay, you can stop with the jokes now. You've had better. I get it. No need to rub it in." She stood to grab plates and forks from the cabinet.

"What if I'm not joking?" Levi took the plates and forks from her and laid them on the table.

"Don't even go there. I know you too well." Rhi sat back down and loaded her plate with food. "What do you want to do after lunch?"

"Kiss you some more?"

"Okay, stop." Rhi held up her hand. "You're giving me a complex about my kissing ability."

"I was being serious, Rhi."

She shook her head. She couldn't take it anymore.

"But what if—"

"Freeze. We're done. No more talking about the kiss or any real or joking feelings associated with it."

"Freeze it is." Levi nodded and ran a hand through his hair. "You wanna finish the movie after lunch?"

"Sure." Rhi turned her attention to her plate. "Things aren't going to change between us now, are they?"

"Of course not. We're still friends. Nothing is going to change that. I just know I like to kiss you now."

Rhi tapped her fingers on the counter. He couldn't be serious about anything, but that was one of the things she loved about him. She shoved the plate away and reached for another container. "I think it's a dessert first kind of day."

Levi opened his mouth to say something but smiled instead. "Me too."

MAY 31ST

Levi draped his arm around a bottle blonde whose name he could not remember.

She played with the buttons on his shirt then stood on her toes to press a kiss to his neck.

This was his first date in two weeks. He wouldn't have gone, but Rhi had said something about checking out one of her Tinder matches. He'd be turned on in short enough order, but the chemistry wasn't there. Was this how he wanted to go through the rest of his life? He raked his other hand through his hair.

"You're so hot. How are you still single?"

"Confirmed bachelor usually turns everyone off." Levi folded his arms across his chest.

She ran her fingers over his arms and down to his stomach. "No one is a confirmed bachelor forever. There's always one."

Yeah, her name's Rhi, and she lives with me. Levi shook his head. *Nope, not thinking like that. She's my best friend. Always will be.* He smiled down at the girl as the elevator

96

stopped at his floor. He put his arm around her as they stepped into the hallway, his smile quickly fading.

Rhi stood outside their door with another man, laughing at something he had said.

Levi glowered, and his body heated. He cleared his throat. "I thought you were gone for the night."

"We decided to come here instead." Rhi met his gaze and mouthed, "help."

Levi scowled.

"Who the hell is she?" The blonde planted her hands on her hips.

"This is my wife. We've got an open relationship." Levi put his arm around Rhi. "Monogamy got boring, so we're trying to pick up random people to meet our needs."

The guy with Rhi checked out the blonde. "I'm down. As long as there's no dick touching. Not into guys."

Levi crossed his arms. "You won't be in charge. If Rhi breaks out the whips and chains, we'll all be hanging from the ceiling before too long."

Rhi reached out and pinched the blonde's wrist. "She's a little skinny. Are you sure she'll hang up?"

"I don't know. Did you print the waivers this morning? I forgot."

The blonde pulled away from Rhi and stomped to the elevator. "Everyone at the bar is going to know exactly what kind of person you are, Levi." She pressed the down button repeatedly.

"Everyone at the bar already knows." Levi turned to look at the guy. "Still in? We have waivers in the apartment. I'll try not to touch you, but when you're rolling around in spaghetti sauce, things get confusing."

"Spaghetti sauce?" The man raised his brows.

Rhi nodded. "Yeah, the whole place is lined with plastic. Between the spaghetti sauce and the blood, it gets messy in there."

The man raced to the elevator as it opened for the blonde. "Hey! Wait up." He climbed onto the elevator.

Rhi opened the apartment door. "Thanks. You didn't have to ruin your date too though."

He shrugged. "It wasn't going anywhere. She's determined to change me from a bachelor to a husband."

"Women can't seem to get that through their head, can they?" She chuckled as she hastened inside. "Thanks again for the save. I'm going to bed. If you go out and need cover again, text me." She plodded toward her room.

Levi closed the door behind him. "Rhi."

"What?" She turned to look at him.

His eyes blurred, and he let his imagination take hold. He strode across the room, backed her against the wall, and planted a hot kiss on her lips. "There's only one person I want tonight and you're her."

"What?" Rhi snapped her fingers in front of his face. "Levi."

He shook the vision out of his head and forced a smile. "Sorry. Must still be tired."

"Who were you talking to?" Rhi walked over to him and put her hand on his shoulder. "You sure you're okay?"

"Yeah, fine." He took a deep breath. "Hey, your dad texted me earlier and said they're going to the island on June eighth and asked if I wanted to go."

"Good. We can go together. I won't have to fly with the twins then."

"We're not going to all ride in the same vehicle to the airport? Big family van like we did in school?"

"No. No way." Rhi shook her head. "We'll leave a little earlier and arrive before them."

"I'll book the flights. First class to spoil you as usual." Levi laughed and headed to his room.

He checked the text from her dad to book the flight. His mind drifted back to Rhi. He wanted to have a serious conversation with her, but every time he tried, she thought he was joking. He exhaled as his phone chimed.

LEON:

If you're coming on vacation with us, I want to discuss my offer.

LEVI:

I'll be there. I'm very interested.

LEON:

Good. I'm working through the legal aspects and should have a contract to go through while we're there.

Levi smiled. Owner of a company at twenty-four. How many of his friends could say that?

LEVI:

I'm ready.

He rushed through the flight plans.

Her door was closed, and he knocked before he walked in.

Rhi stood in her room dressed only in her lacy peach bra and matching panties. "What's the point of knocking if you're just going to come in?"

Levi stared at her, his gaze raking over her curves. His body heated and he swallowed hard.

Rhi grabbed her robe from the bed and wrapped it around her. "Why are you looking at me like that?"

"I…um." He and shook his head. "I wanted to tell you the good news first."

"Tell me." She plopped down on the bed and patted the comforter next to her.

Levi's mind went blank. What was he going to tell her? He couldn't get the image of her half naked out of his head. He cleared his throat and sat down. "Your dad said he'd be drawing up a contract for me to take over the company."

Rhi threw her arms around his neck. "That's amazing! I'm so proud of you."

Levi returned the gesture, relishing the feel of her against him. He fought the desire to kiss her. "Rhi?"

"What?"

He took her by the shoulders and held her away from him. He was never going to get through this conversation with her close enough that he could smell her shampoo. "Would you consider changing our relationship? Don't answer right now. Give it until we leave for vacation. But I can't stop thinking about our kiss."

"Is it just a sex thing? You want to do friends with benefits? Or more? You remind me frequently of your confirmed bachelor status."

"Think about both. Because I know I have been."

"You? *You're* considering more than one night…and monogamy?" Rhi quirked her brow.

"I've never been monogamously challenged. Only one girl at a time."

Rhi took a deep breath. "What about our friendship? It will change."

"I know. But I can't stop thinking it already has. The moment we started talking about kissing something changed."

"Are you sure you don't want to talk about this now?"

He shook his head. "I can't. I'll call a limited freeze if I need to, but if we start now, we will end up in bed."

She looked around. "We're in bed right now."

"You know what I mean."

"You're trying to be funny again, aren't you?"

Levi tipped her head back and moved his lips over hers in a quick but sensual kiss. "I'm not kidding, Rhi." He pulled away from her, stood up, and raced out of the room. His head spun. *What the hell did I just do?*

Chapter Seventeen

Rhi

JUNE 4TH

R hi paced back and forth across her brother's living room. The wait was killing her.

Edge glanced up from his phone. "How am I supposed to sell this house if you make a hole in my floor?"

Rhi growled and plopped down in the chair next to the couch. "Why did he have to call a temporary freeze? He knows I won't say anything about it until he calls it off. But no. Now I'm stuck waiting until the damn ride to the fucking airport."

"Going somewhere?"

"Did you turn dumb on me? We're leaving for vacation in four days. Four of the longest days ever. Well, after the last five long ass days I've been through." She threw her hands in the air. "Freeze! Damn it. Why?"

"Tell him you love him and get it over with. Freeze or not, I'm pretty sure 'I love you' beats it."

She stared at her brother. "You don't even know who I'm talking about. Why in the world would you tell me to tell some stranger I love them?"

He stood, walked over to her, and put his hands on her shoulders. "Levi. You're talking about Levi."

Rhi blew out a deep breath. "Why does kissing your best friend have to complicate everything?"

Edge smiled. "Because you're at the point you realize you were too young to recognize love when you first met."

"I don't think I'm in love with him. At least not in the romantic way." Rhi looked over at him. "How did you and Sara do it?"

"I started looking at the things we were doing as friends and realized it was what I wanted in a relationship. I looked at my other relationships and saw they weren't good for me."

"You were all of sixteen when you and Sara got together. You told me she was your first and only." Rhi picked at her nails.

"I'd dated a couple girls before her. They couldn't deal with my friendship with Sara, and they didn't have the same ideas I had when it came to a relationship. I wanted someone I could trust implicitly. Someone I could spend days with and not get tired of them. Someone I could have comfortable silence with. Someone I could be myself around and not have to pretend to be something I wasn't. You can't tell me that's not what you have with Levi."

"The person you can eat whatever you want in front of them and not have to worry about them thinking it's not feminine. The one who's always there for me. The one who'll lay on the couch with me and watch stupid movies until we both fall asleep. Or who can order my favorites from any takeout place without asking what I wanted." Rhi smiled.

"You can tell them anything. They'll drop everything to do something with you."

"The guy who kicks everyone at his party out of the apartment so he can come in and make me feel better. Or who rescues me when the woman I thought was a good friend tried to rob me blind."

"To be fair, if you'd called me, I would have come for the last one. And the police would have handled it differently." Edge laughed as he sat down again. "And while all of that is friendship, it can be so much more as well."

"We've always said we were going to live with each other forever and no one was going to break us up."

"If you're a couple, no one can break you up."

Rhi nodded. "I want to tell him I want to try the whole dating thing now, but he wants me to think about it until we go on vacation."

"He may be thinking about things as well. He needs his own time to make sure this is what he wants. To talk to his friends and family. This will be a big change for him. He's never done more than one date. He's been a confirmed bachelor for so long, it has to be weird for him to think about being in a relationship."

"I guess you're right. Waiting the last five days has been hell. I want to tell him so much, but he's barely been around."

"From what I understand, he's also getting ready to take over Dad's company and move back to Bryton. I'm sure there are a few other things he needs to get figured out."

Rhi smiled at her brother. "You're right, as much as I hate to admit it. I need to give him his time too. It's probably as hard on him as it is on me."

"Exactly."

She yawned. "I suppose I should go see if I can bunk in my old room tonight. I'm not feeling up to driving back to Indy."

"We have extra rooms and I know Sara will have more insight into your plight than I do. You're more than welcome to stay here."

Rhi glanced over at him and nodded. "Thank you. I guess it would be better. Otherwise Mom's going to drag it all out of me."

"You bet she will." Edge pointed to the stairs. "There's three bedrooms upstairs. Make yourself at home."

Rhi stood and opened her arms to Edge. "I came to talk to Sara, but I think you were the one I needed to talk to."

"Sometimes older brothers know a thing or two." He hugged her tight and released her. "Get some sleep, sis. And wake up knowing your life will be changing from this point forward."

She smiled and rushed up the stairs. He was right. Her life would be changing.

JUNE 5TH

L evi pulled up in front of his father's house on the outskirts of Bryton. He climbed out of the car and hurried to the house. He opened the door and stepped into the living room. A mismatched array of thrift store furniture filled the room. "Hey, Dad?"

"Levi." Fletcher Morris walked out of the kitchen and over to hug his son. "What brings you up my way? No date on a Friday night?"

"Not tonight."

Fletcher raised his eyebrows. "You have them all planned out for tomorrow and Sunday then?"

"Nah, Rhi and I leave for the island on Monday, so I'll be packing." Levi shoved his hands in his pockets. How long had it been since he'd been on a date that didn't end early?

"Well, shit, son. You're slowing down. How am I supposed to live vicariously through you if you don't have a new girl every night?" Fletcher laughed and motioned for him to follow. "I'm working on a new recipe."

"Torturing food again, Dad?"

Fletcher shot him a glare. "I'm getting better."

The smell of garlic and Italian seasonings wafted through the air.

"Smells all right." Levi sat down at the kitchen table. "I stopped by to talk to you about something."

"Oh yeah? What's that?" Fletcher stirred the pot of food on the stove.

"Leon Edgerly contacted me about a possible job opportunity." Levi focused on his hands. "He wants me to take over his part of the company."

Fletcher turned and smiled at his son. "That's one helluva opportunity."

Levi nodded. "I know. He's not retiring yet, and he'll be around to help me out and get everything settled."

"Congratulations, son. I'm proud of you. How long before this goes into effect? A couple years?"

Levi's cheeks heated. "We're going over the contracts next week. I gave my two weeks' notice today. I'm spending the next month finding a place to live up here so I can get started by the end of the summer."

Fletcher leaned against the counter. "That was quick. What's with waiting to tell your old man?"

"I didn't want to just call you up and tell you. I wanted to come up here and tell you in person."

"If it wasn't for Leon and Jen, I'd still be working in a factory, trying to make ends meet." Fletcher turned around and stirred the contents in the pot.

"I know." Levi smiled. He'd spent many a night at the Edgerly house while his dad was going to school.

"You're excited about taking over the company, right?"

"Yeah." He sighed.

"Something else seems to be bothering you." He turned off the stove, grabbed a couple bowls, and put them on the table. "I have some noodles in the fridge. Can you get them for me?"

Levi found the bag of noodles and handed them to his dad. "There's nothing bothering me. I'm just overwhelmed."

"I understand. Everything always happens fast with the Edgerlys. They have the money to get things done and they tend to do it." He put the cold noodles in both bowls and spooned the tomato-based sauce over them. "The sauce should warm them up."

"Makes sense to me, but every time I do that, Rhi rolls her eyes." Levi shrugged.

"How is Rhi? I haven't seen her in a while." Fletcher sat down. "Sit. Try it."

Levi sat then stirred the sauce into the noodles, waiting a moment before he took a bite. "Not bad, Dad. Not bad at all."

"Rhi or the food?"

Levi laughed. "The food is good. And Rhi, well, I guess she's okay. I haven't talked to her much the last few days."

"You live with her. The woman has spent the last seventeen years taking out the trash after your one-night stands. What do you mean you haven't talked to her?"

"I've been trying to finish up projects at my current job so I can quit and not leave them hanging. I've been working pretty late." *And you've been avoiding her.*

"That's the biggest load of crock I've ever heard." His

dad shook his head. "Sounds more like you've been avoiding her."

Levi frowned. *When did Dad become psychic?* "I'm not *avoiding* her per se."

"Right. Cough it up. What happened between you two?"

"Well, you see…" He spent the next ten minutes catching his dad up on everything that had happened. "And after I told her to think about it until we left. Then I realized it meant I had to do the same. I've dug through feelings I didn't know I had. I tried going on dates and that didn't work. I think I'm ready to tell her I want to try this dating thing with her, but I'm also trying to give her the time I told her I would."

"It's about damn time you two figured out you need to be more than friends. Jen, Leon, and I have been saying this forever."

Levi chuckled. "You're not the only ones. I just…"

Fletcher put his hand on his son's and gave it a gentle squeeze. "It's okay to be scared about this. You're having feelings you've never had before. Let's face it, you're stepping into a situation you've never been in before."

"I've dated plenty, Dad."

"Take every one-night stand out you've had. *Have* you dated?"

Levi racked his brain, trying to remember the last time he'd been on a second or third date. "Probably not. I don't even think I dated girls in high school longer than one date. I had my best friend. The only thing I needed from other girls was sex."

"Take the time you've given yourself. Work through

what you need to work through. When you get on the plane, tell her how you feel."

"Thanks, Dad. You're right." Levi smiled. "Hopefully this doesn't backfire."

JUNE 8TH

R hi answered Levi's call with the hands-free device on her steering wheel. "Please tell me you're still coming."

"I just got here. I was calling to find out if *you* were still coming."

"How did we end up heading to the airport with the family again?"

"Your dad canceled our plane tickets because he didn't want us to pay for it." Levi chuckled.

"Great, a three-hour drive to Chicago with my sisters and a six-year-old."

"I'm not sure Milo's coming. He's not here."

She pulled into the driveway. "I'm here now."

"See you in a minute." Levi disconnected the call.

She opened the door as her phone rang again. "Hey. I'll be right in."

"Where are you? I need you at the office."

Rhi looked at her phone. "Oh, hi, Delilah. I'm at my parents' house right now. We're leaving for the airport in less than an hour."

"What the hell do you mean you're leaving? Where are you going?"

"I told you this last week when I asked for my vacation time. My family owns an island in the Caribbean. I'm going with my family and Levi."

"Levi. Right. The friend you're moving an hour a way for." Delilah let out a heavy breath. "Listen, I have a ninety-day social media marketing plan I need to get started the moment you get back. No questions asked. It's already put together. You just have to schedule and/or post it and keep up with the messages. If you could check the sites while you're on vacation, that would be even better. I don't want to miss any potential business."

"Why would you put together a social media plan without consulting me? Isn't that what I was hired to do?" Rhi scowled and hit the steering wheel of her car. *God, she infuriates me.*

"I hired you to do the posting and responding. I don't *need* your help with social media. That's my job."

Rhi growled. "Are you serious? I freaking spent four years in college doing social media marketing research about what sells and what doesn't and you're telling me it's not my job? Do you even know what goes into making a marketing plan? The hours?"

"This isn't my first rodeo. I know what I'm doing, and I put this plan together. This is my company, and you'll do what I say. Not what you want to do. You want to do something else, go find another job."

Rhi screamed in her head. "Fine. But I'm not working while we're on vacation. I'll be back in the office next Tuesday, ready to start your marketing plan."

"Good. No working from home either. I need you *physically* in the office for this plan to succeed."

Rhi rolled her eyes. "Fine, whatever. I'll be there."

"Good." Delilah hung up the phone.

She hit her steering wheel again, took a deep breath, and fled into the madhouse. A hand grasped her arm and pulled her into a tight embrace in the dark foyer. Levi's scent enveloped her, and she nestled into his chest. "I've missed you."

"Me too." Levi kissed her head. "I can't wait to be done with all this and talk."

"Why'd we have to ride with them?" Rhi groaned. "I wanted to spend time with you. Especially after you were gone the last three days."

"I needed to sort some things out. And I wanted to give you some alone time to think things through too."

She grasped his shirt. "I didn't need the extra time. I made my decision."

Levi moved her away from him. "Tell me what you decided."

Mason stepped into the foyer and motioned for them to follow. "Hey, Rhi. Levi. Get in here. Mom's ready to go."

Levi moaned. "Can you give us a minute?"

"Mom said I'm not allowed to leave you two until you follow me." Mason bounced on his heels and looked everywhere but at the two of them.

Levi growled. "Fine. Maybe we'll have a moment to ourselves on the plane."

"Doubtful." Rhi took a step away from him and turned to follow Mason.

"Glad you two could join us." Jen grinned. "Mason,

you're in the back with Lex, Chelsea, and Kym. Rhi and Levi in the next seat, Dad and I will be in the front row 'cause Edge is driving."

Kym rolled her eyes. "Mom, we haven't needed seating charts since Elementary school."

Jen laughed. "Right. Okay, fine. Pick your own then. We'll see how it works. Suitcases are packed. Let's go."

Rhi pointed toward the door. "Mine are in my trunk."

"I got them out while you were talking to Levi in the foyer." Edge patted her on the shoulder and headed out to the van.

"Where's Milo?" Rhi glanced over at Sara.

"Staying with Aunt Sandie. The family seems to think we need grown-up time." Sara chuckled.

"Go on. I'll let you all choose your seats then take whatever's left." Kym plopped down on the couch and crossed her legs, batting her eyes at Levi.

Levi put his arm around Rhi, turned her to the door, and walked outside. "Would have worked out better if we'd gone with your mom's seating chart."

"Right? Kym's totally going to be with us now." Rhi clenched her teeth as she climbed into the van, sitting in the middle of the row. "She's not out here yet. Maybe we'll get lucky."

Levi sat in the aisle seat and leaned close to her ear. "I upgraded us to first class. We should have some alone time on the plane."

"Come on, Levi. You know we have no secrets here." Kym beamed at him and motioned for them to move. "I have to sit by the window or I get car sick."

Rhi pointed over her shoulder. "The window seat behind us is wide open and so is the one in front of us."

"Yeah, I'm not sitting back there and watching Chelsea and Lex make out the entire time."

"If it makes you feel better, I can make out with Rhi the whole way." Levi grinned and climbed out of the van.

Kym smirked at Rhi and climbed over her to the window seat. She patted the seat next to her and beckoned for Levi to sit down. "Move over, Rhi."

Rhi shook her head. "Nope. Levi will be more comfortable on the outside. Deal with it."

Jen groaned. "Just get in the damn van!"

"Yes, ma'am!" Levi hopped back into his seat and shut the door.

Kym glared at her sister and folded her arms over her chest.

Rhi blew out a deep breath. *This is going to be the longest three hours ever.*

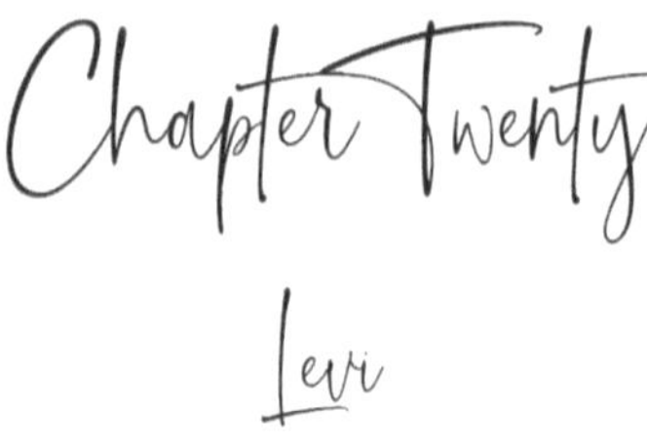

Chapter Twenty

Levi

While he waited for Rhi to finish chatting with her parents, Levi stretched out in his seat in first class.

A woman and a young girl walked over and sat in the two seats in front of them.

The little girl turned in her seat and stared at him. "Why are you alone?"

"My girlfriend is talking to someone she knows in the main cabin."

"Sit down, honey." The mother patted the girl on her shoulder.

"No, I want to sit next to him." She pointed back to Levi.

"Honey, this is our row. He has someone traveling with him."

The little girl stood in the aisle and stamped her feet. "I want to sit there." She motioned to Rhi's seat.

"Caroline, you're not going to get your way this time." Her mother stood and took the girl's arm.

Levi leaned toward the mother and whispered in her ear. "Let her sit there. You and I can change seats when my girlfriend arrives."

The mother smiled at him. "Thanks." She turned to her daughter. "Okay, honey. This nice man has agreed to let you sit there."

Caroline beamed and hopped into the seat next to Levi.

Rhi walked into first class and frowned at the girl in her seat. "Was there a mistake in booking?"

"It's all been figured out. You're sitting right up there." He gestured to the seat next to the girl's mother.

She stood up. "Sorry about this."

"Ohhkay." Rhi sat down in the other seat.

Levi rose and changed places with the mother. "The little girl wanted to sit there, so we all switched."

"Okayyyy." Rhi chuckled. "Even the little ones like you."

"Yeah, no. I'm not one for kids."

"Good."

Rhi jumped. "She's got a sharp kick."

Levi tilted his head to see Caroline standing and kicking the back of Rhi's seat.

"Ma'am." He motioned to her daughter.

"Oh, I'm sorry." She grabbed her daughter and put her back in her seat. "I'm Charlotte, by the way."

Rhi snuggled into Levi's. "Are we going to talk about what we decided?"

"We are." He kissed her head.

"Ladies and gentlemen, the captain has turned the

fasten seatbelt light on." The flight attendant announced through the speaker.

"But not now." He blew out a breath.

"Shhhh," Caroline shushed them. "The lady is talking," she shouted.

Rhi giggled.

As soon as the plane took off, Caroline sobbed loud enough that everyone in first class turned to look. This lasted until the seatbelt light went off and the flight attendant announced they could move about the cabin. Caroline was out of her seat and in Levi's lap in less than a minute. "I wanna sit with you."

"You can't sit on my lap, and this other seat is taken." Levi put his hands up so the least amount of him was touching the little girl.

"I want it and I'm going to scream until I get it." She let out a blood-curdling wail, which caused the flight attendants to rush toward them.

"What's wrong, honey?" Charlotte picked up her daughter off Levi's lap and cuddled her close, causing the noise to intensify.

"I want to sit next to him." Caroline wriggled out of her mother's arms then stomped her feet.

One of the flight attendants touched her shoulder. "You need to sit in your own seat, young lady."

Caroline screamed louder. "I want to sit by *him*."

Levi sank down in his seat. "And this is the reason I want nothing to do with kids."

"You and me both." Rhi covered her ears.

"Sir, would it be all right if she sits next to you?"

Levi's eyes grew wide. "You're not serious, are you?

You'd let your little kid sit next to a stranger?"

"I'm right here, and I think everyone on the plane would be grateful if she stopped."

Rhi shook her head. "Guess we'll have our conversation later." She moved past Levi and into the seat next to Charlotte.

Levi exhaled and motioned for Caroline to sit down. How many times had he been on a plane with Rhi's parents? Jen and Leon would never have allowed their children to act like that.

Caroline gave him a big grin, plopped down beside him, and leaned on his arm. "Sometimes I get boogers… and I eat them."

"Ma'am." Levi looked for a flight attendant.

"Yes, sir?"

"I upgraded my girlfriend and I to first class, but I can't do this. Can you upgrade someone else so we can go back to business class?"

"No!" Caroline shouted. "I want to sit with *you!*"

Levi stood. "Nope, sorry. I'm not risking a little girl or her mother making any kind of claims against me just to make sure she stops screaming."

The flight attendant turned to Charlotte. "He's right. I don't want that liability either. You're going to have to take your daughter back to your seats."

"She's going to yell the entire flight if she doesn't get what she wants."

"That's on you. I'll take your seat so you don't have to move her."

Her mother nodded and took his seat.

Caroline started screaming as soon as her mother sat

down.

The flight attendant looked at Charlotte. "If she can't calm down before we begin takeoff, we'll have to ask you to take a later flight."

Levi took the seat next to Rhi. "This is going to be the longest flight ever."

"That's what I thought about the ride here."

"Agreed. Why didn't we fly private?" Levi rested his head back against the seat.

"The plane was out for maintenance and Mom and Dad figured it would just be easier to fly commercial." Rhi cocked her head and gave him a slight smile. "Did you just call me your girlfriend?"

"I did."

"Does that mean that's your decision?"

Caroline turned around in her seat and glared at Rhi. "I hate you!" She let out another blood-curdling scream.

They both covered their ears.

"Caroline!" Her mother pulled her back into her seat. "We can't get kicked off this plane. You need to be quiet."

"Yes, but let's talk when we get to the island. There's no telling what kind of issues we'll have before we get there."

Rhi sighed and leaned her head against him. "We can't get there fast enough."

JUNE 8TH

The moon shone through the window as Rhi stretched out on the king-sized bed. Every time they visited Edgerly Island, they stayed in the same private residence.

There was a knock on her door.

"Come in." She rolled onto her back and scooted herself up until she was sitting against the headboard.

Levi smiled. "Hey."

"Come sit down and talk to me." She patted the spot beside her.

He climbed onto the bed next to Rhi. "That was a crazy trip."

"I don't think my eardrums will ever recover from the terror name Caroline. I'm just glad she fell asleep on the second leg of our trip." She rubbed her ears.

"It was hilarious when your mom gave her *the* look at the airport during the layover. She was fairly quiet after that."

"Until we got back on the plane."

Levi put his arm around her and kissed her head. "So, we're dating."

"Did you ask me what I thought about the whole situation or are we just going with your decision?" She chuckled.

"I mean, if your decision is the same as mine, then yes. If not, well, you're wrong and I may need to kiss you until you agree with me." He grinned.

Rhi smacked him in the chest. "You're an ass."

"You wouldn't have me any other way though."

"I agree with you about us dating now, but I have questions."

"Questions about what?"

"If we do the friends with benefits thing, are we still going to be sleeping with other people?"

Levi opened his mouth to respond, but Rhi held her hand up.

"What happens if it doesn't work out? What if we suck in bed together? What if there isn't any chemistry?"

"You can't say there's no chemistry. My whole body tingles every time you touch me." Levi slid his fingers down her arm. "Tell me you don't feel something?"

"Well, of course I do. My body gets hot, and I want to kiss you like crazy." She laughed. "Okay, so maybe there's *some* chemistry, but what about—"

Levi lowered her onto the bed then swept his tongue across her lip, meeting hers in a sensuous dance.

Rhi moaned. "What was that for?"

"You're cute when you think too much." He smoothed her hair and sat up. "I don't want to sleep with anyone else if we're going to do this. Either way, I want it to be just us."

"Then why even mention friends with benefits? That doesn't suggest exclusivity."

"True. But the idea of calling it a relationship is scary." He rolled off of her then held his arm out.

Rhi rolled her eyes and snuggled against him. "That's because you've never had one.

"Are we going to do this or not?"

She kissed his cheek. "Well, of course we are."

"If we're going to do this, I want to start out slow."

"Then let's skip the relationship and just do friends with benefits."

"Nope. I don't just want to jump into bed with you."

"We're in bed now…again."

"You know what I mean."

"What are you thinking? Fancy dates?"

"Remember when we were talking about them making a romantic comedy about our lives? The same things we normally do. Just with kissing and the possibility of it leading to sex?"

Rhi scowled. "Damn it. I hate it when you're right."

"You up for pizza, beer, and hours of home improvement shows on TV?"

"We're on a private island with the ocean just a few feet away and you want to do the same thing we do every day?"

"Uh uh. Food is out because I'm stuffed from dinner. How about beer and a walk on the beach?"

"That's more like it." She gave him a wide smile. "Are we *really* doing this?"

"We are."

"I guess you should get the beer then." She pushed him gently and sat up.

"Wait. Aren't you supposed to bring me my beer after a hard day of work while I relax?" He smiled as he got to his feet.

"If we're enforcing gender stereotypes, I guess you're paying for everything now and I can stay home and raise the kids."

"If by kids you mean cats, I'm cool with that. If you're talking about miniature versions of you and me, no."

She folded her arms across her chest. "Well, I guess I can't get your beer."

"Keep doing that. It pushes up your boobs." He laughed and bolted out of her room.

Rhi rolled her eyes and walked to the double doors that led out to the patio. The moon was bright and shimmered off the pool.

RHI:

Put your swim trunks on and meet me outside.

She went into the bathroom and quickly changed into her teal and white bikini with the tie front, stopping at her suitcase to grab her black lace kimono coverup. She breezed through the living area and out onto the terrace.

Soft lighting came on the moment she stepped outside. Oversized wicker furniture was spread out over the terrace, covered in comfortable linen cushions. The marble tile continued from the house to the terrace and down the path that led to the pool.

Rhi sat on one of the wicker chairs to wait for Levi, but she didn't have to wait long.

He handed Rhi a bottle and set his on the table next to her chair.

She jumped when his cold hands landed on her shoulders, working out the knots that appeared on the plane.

"You're not as tense as you were the last time I did this."

"I wasn't in paradise with the man of my dreams after he admitted he wanted to date me." She glanced up at him then took a swig of her beer.

"Well, damn. I guess I need to step out of the way." He walked around the chair and offered her his hand. "I'd hate to get in the way of the man of your dreams."

Rhi smiled as she let him pull her to her feet. "What if *you're* the man of my dreams?"

Levi pulled her close. "I'll have to get used to it."

She rested her head against his bare chest. A flush of warmth rushed through her entire body. She was blissfully aware of their nearness. His embrace was different than before. The lines of the muscles of his chest. His strong arms. He toyed with her hair and traced a line down her back, leaving flames in his wake.

"Levi?" She tilted her head to look into his eyes.

He drew his fingers from her wrists to her shoulders then cupped her neck, lowering his lips to hers. The kiss was slow at first. Her lips parted, and his tongue toyed with hers in a dance.

The thin fabric between them did little to hide his growing arousal.

She moaned. "I want you." Her voice was raspy.

Levi kissed her one more time before pulling away. "Being good is going to be harder than I thought."

She clutched his arms, not sure her knees would hold her. "Then why fight it? We've never been ones for conventional relationships, so why do it with us?"

Levi cupped her cheek. "Because you're special. Because I want this to be real, not some crazy five-month friends with benefits thing that ends with us hating each other. I want you to know how serious about this I am."

Rhi hugged him. "You puddled me."

"I *what?*"

"My heart melted to the floor and the rest of me followed. You have a puddle of Rhi at your feet."

Levi laughed. "That's gross and hilarious all at the same time." He took a step away and grasped her hand. "Walk on the beach or dip in the pool?"

"Cold shower alone would be smarter." Rhi gave him a sly smile.

"The outdoor shower looks like a lot of fun."

"That would lead us somewhere you don't want to go."

"Walk on the beach?"

Rhi squeezed his hand as they strolled toward the white sands. "Perfect."

"Yes, you are."

Chapter Twenty-Two

Levi

Levi stood in the shower, hoping the cold water would cool the flames that raged through him every time he was with Rhi. He wanted this to work but didn't want to rush.

He turned off the water and toweled dry before putting his shorts on and heading into his bedroom.

Rhi sat on his bed, dressed in her bikini and sheer coverup.

Damn. So much for the cold shower.

She smiled. "Mom says they're cooking in the main house if you're interested in eating with the fam."

"I was thinking of a date instead." Levi plopped down beside her. "We spent the whole day with the family. I want some alone time with you."

"Are we going to tell them about us dating? Or are we going to let them figure it out?"

"I have an idea. You go over to the main house. Tell them you have a date for dinner, then I'll show up." Levi laughed. "Your parents would enjoy the joke."

"Probably." Rhi bumped his arm with hers. "Where are we going?"

"I made reservations at the Boathouse. Figured it was close enough and still fancy enough."

"Sounds perfect. Let me go change."

"Meet you at the main house in about an hour?" He pressed a soft kiss on her lips then moved over to his suitcase.

"Hey, I forgot to tell you about the call I got from Delilah before we left."

"Oh yeah?" He turned around, holding a pair of khaki shorts.

"We've been so busy. I haven't had time to tell you." She wrung her hands together.

"Hey." Levi sat down and put his arms around her. "What happened? Something bad?"

"Apparently, she put together this big ninety-day marketing plan and expects me to be in the office first thing Monday to start setting it up. She didn't even run it by me…just did it by herself. Said she's the marketing expert and I just do the social media posting. She tried to demand I work on vacation too."

"Quit. You don't need that kind of crap. You didn't spend four years of college learning about marketing to only post on social media." He kissed her cheek.

"I can't quit. Especially not if we're moving. Too many expenses. What happens if I can't find a job in Bryton? I'm not gonna ask you to take care of me."

Levi put his hands on her shoulders and held her at arm's length. "You have a large trust fund. You could live off the interest and never have to work again. I understand you want to work, but not having a job shouldn't be your biggest worry. We'll be fine. And it's not like your parents wouldn't help if we did get into a jam."

She sighed. "They didn't raise me that way though. I need to be able to do this on my own. I don't want to rely on other people."

"Isn't that one of the best parts of a relationship? Being able to rely on the other person?" His hands slid down her arms and squeezed her hands. "I'm gonna support you no matter what. If you want to quit, quit. We'll make it work. If you want to stay working for her, that's fine too, but don't let yourself be beaten down by a boss who doesn't respect you."

Rhi gave him a half smile and a quick kiss. "We should have done this dating thing a long time ago."

"I know." Levi grinned. "Now go get dressed so we can go mess with your parents."

She stood up, gave him a slight wave, and scurried out of the room.

Levi picked up his khaki shorts, a light blue button-down shirt, and his brown leather sandals. He combed his hair back and went back into his room to check the time. *Great...still have fifty-five minutes to kill.* He texted Rhi.

LEVI:

Let me know when you're over there.

He turned on the television and searched for something to watch.

Ten minutes later, he still hadn't found anything worth staying on for long. He checked his phone. Nothing from Rhi either.

LEVI:

Everything okay?

RHI:

At the main house getting ready. You gave
me an hour. I'm using all of it. 😌

LEVI:

All right. I'll try to be patient.

He groaned and flipped through the channels again before turning the TV off and heading outside. *Maybe a walk on the beach will help.*

Edge walked down the path that led to the beach.

Levi jogged over to him. "Care if I join you?"

"Not at all. My wife is helping your girlfriend pick an outfit."

"Wait, she told you?"

"Yes, and she stopped by the house a few days ago while you two were avoiding each other." Edge chuckled.

"I guess that makes sense. I didn't think she'd go to your mom."

"I'm sure she would have if I didn't give her the answer she wanted."

Levi looked at Edge. "You're not upset that your dad is offering me his part of the company, are you?"

"Hell no. Dad tried to teach me software development when I was in high school. I tried to like it, but I finally had to tell him I had no interest in it. Plus, we really like it in Minnesota, so taking over a company in Bryton is kinda out."

"How's the house sale going?"

"I don't know. Part of me wants to keep it, but we're

not in town enough to warrant that." He sighed and glanced over at Levi. "Are you interested in a house rather than an apartment?"

"Your place is pretty big. Rhi and I are thinking our kids are going to be feline, so I can't even imagine what we'd do with all that room."

"Home offices, host parties. That's what we did. There's even a guest suite with a separate entrance if you want a friend to live with you for a while." Edge shrugged.

"I'll have to talk it over with Rhi."

"Yeah, I'd hope so. I wasn't suggesting you make that decision on your own. I just know you two are looking at places when we get back to Bryton."

Levi looked out over the beach. *Do I really want the responsibility of a house? Am I ready for that?* "When do you need an answer?"

"We're sticking around another two or three weeks before we head back to Harper's Crossing, so that's when it will officially go up for sale. I took two months off in case something caused a delay."

"That's a helluva job if you can do that."

"I'm good at what I do. When they call, I answer any questions they need, and I have access to a lab in Bryton if they need me to do anything. This is the only week I'm on full vacation."

"I'll think about it and see what Rhi says."

"Tell her I'll give it to you two if she wants it. That way she doesn't have to bug Mom about using the trust fund." Edge bumped his shoulder.

"You're really sweetening the deal there." He laughed.

"If you're not interested, I won't push. I just thought I'd offer."

Levi nodded as they turned to head back toward the house. His mind raced. His life had changed drastically over the past few months. *I'm actually dating one woman for the first time...ever...and my best friend at that. I have a helluva job opportunity, and I'm moving, possibly into a house. None of those were even thoughts in my head two months ago.*

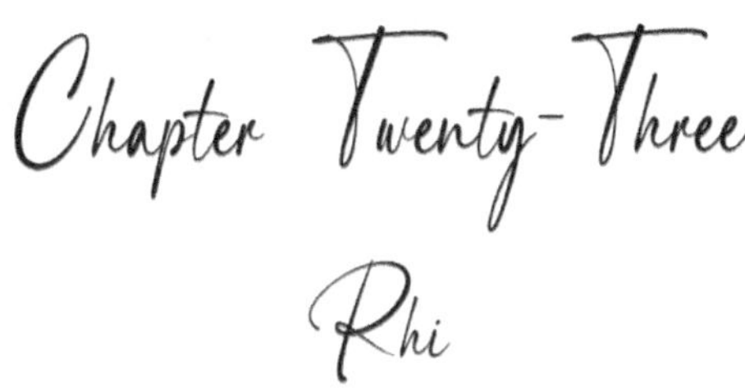

JUNE 9TH

"You have to help me." Rhi dropped a bunch of dresses on Sara's bed.

Sara shook her head as she sorted through the pile. "How many dates are you going on?"

"Just one. But it has to be *perfect*."

"Why? It's Levi. He's seen you when you first wake up. You don't have to be perfect around him."

"But it's our first date and I want it to be special." Rhi picked up one of the dresses. Short, blue, lace. Too formal.

"Hon, you're on a private island in the Caribbean. You're going to the fanciest restaurant on said island, and you're with a date, who also happens to be your best friend. How could that get any more special?" Sara put her hands on Rhi's shoulders. "Do you think he's going to care what you wear?"

"Probably not." She scanned the pile of dresses again.

Sara held up a turquoise off-the-shoulder maxi dress with a floral pattern on it. "Here. Not too fancy. Perfect for over a bathing suit but still good enough for the Boathouse."

Rhi took the dress, hugged her sister-in-law, and hurried into the bathroom to change. She brushed her hair and twisted it into an updo. A touch of makeup finished the look then she stepped back out to show Sara.

"You look wonderful. Now, what shoes are you wearing?"

Rhi picked up a pair of gold sandals. "If he decides to walk on the beach later, I'll carry them."

Sara laughed. "Love it."

A knock sounded on the door. "You two coming out for dinner?" Jen called.

Sara opened the door and smiled at Jen. "Rhi's got a date."

"That was quick." Jen turned toward Rhi. "I didn't think you'd have time to find one with all the time you and Levi have spent together. You look amazing."

"Thank you. He's meeting me here in a few minutes." Rhi pulled out her phone to text Levi.

RHI:

Ready when you are.

"I don't think I've met one of your dates since you were in high school."

"Yeah, well, when you kept giving the same safe sex lecture to everyone who walked through the door, it got a little old."

Jen grinned. "Oooh, can I do it again? For old times' sake?"

"Sure, Mom. But make it short."

The doorbell rang and Jen breezed over to open the door. She opened it and gestured for the person to come in. "False alarm, it's just Levi." She smacked his arm. "And since when do you ring the doorbell?"

"Since I'm your daughter's date?" His gaze went to Rhi, and he gaped. "Damn. You look amazing."

Rhi blushed and glanced back at Sara. "Thank you."

"Anytime."

Jen stared at Levi, her mouth hanging open. "You two…are finally more than just friends?"

Rhi smiled at her mother. "Yeah, this is our first real date."

"It's about damn time." Leon smiled from the archway that led to the dining area. "Guess you don't want to talk contracts tonight."

"How about tomorrow?" He looped Rhi's arm through his. "Tonight, we have plenty of plans."

Rhi's face flushed. "We can keep some of them private."

Jen waggled her finger at him. "Now, you two don't do anything I wouldn't do."

Levi chuckled. "From what I've heard that list is pretty short."

Jen snorted. "True. Just remember her pleasure too and you two should be great. Oh, and there's a place between—"

Levi blushed and held his free hand up. "Nope. Don't want to hear it. Rhi, it's time to go."

"Night all." Rhi waved to her family as Levi led her out of the house.

He walked over to the golf cart in front of the villa. "It's kinda weird driving my date around in a golf cart."

"Better than walking…and they're the only vehicles on the island. I'd say we're pretty limited in options."

Levi's eyes grew wide. "Well get in before your mother comes out to try and scar me more."

"We'd both be on the receiving end of that." Rhi sat down in the passenger's seat. "What are these other plans we have?"

"I don't know. We could go for a walk on the beach like we did last night. Or take a dip in the pool?"

"Skinny dipping?"

"Why? We have suits."

Rhi blew out a breath. "You know I'm not shy, though, especially when it comes to sleeping with someone. I've had half as many one-night stands as you have."

"And that's why we're not going there yet. I don't want you to think this is another one-night stand."

"But I know it's not going to be that way. Not with you."

"And if we decide after this date there's nothing more here than friendship? Where do we go from there?" Levi drove the cart down the long driveway and out to the road.

"I guess we go back to being friends." Rhi turned to look at him. "Are you having second thoughts?"

"I don't know. No. Not really."

"We've never kept things from each other before. Let's not start now."

Levi glanced over at her and smiled then turned his attention back to the road. "Let's talk over dinner. I like to be able to look at you when we're talking."

Rhi smiled back. Butterflies swarmed in her stomach. *What if he's having second thoughts? I don't want to go back to being friends. Not when I'm on the brink of knowing what it would be like to be more than friends with him.* The memory of their kiss shot heat through her body. She wanted to feel more. To feel the touch of his skin against hers and more.

Her knee bounced as they got closer to the restaurant.

Levi pulled the golf cart up to the valet area and hurried around to help her down. "Stop worrying." He kissed her cheek.

"How can I not worry when you might be having second thoughts? This could be over before it really begins." She grasped his arms. "Levi, I—"

He covered her mouth with his, his tongue sliding between her parted lips.

Rhi melted into him.

"A private dinner on the beach would be more suitable for that kind of kissing."

Rhi pulled away from Levi, blushing when she turned to see her cousins grinning at her. Liam and Link both wore the official Edgerly Island valet uniform. "Uncle Len finally put you two to work?" Her grandparents owned and still lived on the island, but her Uncle Len ran the day-to-day operations.

Liam shrugged. "I run the entertainment at the resort, and Link's been working to make the island self-sustainable. Hell, all the electricity here is run from solar panels and windmills now. But we also fill in where we're needed." The staff also lived on the island, and when one got sick, there was always someone to fill in.

"That's amazing." Rhi smiled. "You two remember Levi, don't you?"

"How could we not?" Link laughed and shook Levi's

hand. "The three of us got in tons of trouble back in the day."

Liam did the same. "But you two weren't kissing the last time you were here, and I haven't seen the social media queen updating the world on her new relationship status, so is this a hush hush kinda thing?"

"Try more like a brand new kinda thing." Levi chuckled. "This is our first date."

"Well, shit, we're keeping them from doing more than kissing." Link put his arms around their shoulders and led them into the restaurant. "Alban, private family table for these two. This is my cousin Rhi and Levi's her date."

"Pleased to meet you, ma'am and sir." He gave a slight bow. "Right this way."

Rhi and Levi waved to the twins and followed Alban to a private dining area. They stopped in front of a wraparound booth with curtains to block the view of other patrons.

Rhi slid into the back of the booth.

Levi followed and settled in next to her.

Alban handed them menus. "Your waitress will be with you soon. Can I get you drinks?"

"Moscato for Rhi, Cabernet Sauvignon for me."

"Very well." Alban bowed again and disappeared.

Rhi turned in her seat and folded her leg under her. "Are you having second thoughts?"

He took her hands. "I don't want to lose my best friend, but that's not going to stop me from seeing where this goes. I enjoy kissing you too much."

"I can deal with that 'cause I don't know what I'd do without you."

"Are you going to let me order for you?"

Rhi perused the menu. "The maple glazed chicken sounds good."

"Right. You're going to choose a boring chicken breast over steak and lobster?" Levi quirked his brow.

"Well, I mean, when you put it that way." She chuckled. This *was* just Levi. Nothing was going to change except some of what they did together.

"You look amazing." He brushed a stray hair behind her ear.

She blushed. "Thank you."

Levi caressed her cheek. "You never blush with me."

"Yeah, well, you don't usually compliment me like that."

"Well, I should have. You've always been beautiful, Rhi." He kissed her forehead.

The waitress appeared and placed their drinks on the table. "Do you know what you want?"

"We'll both have the steak and lobster, the steak rare. And can we have some unsweetened tea to go with that?" Levi put his arm around Rhi.

"Can I get you anything else?"

"No, we're good. Thank you." Levi gave the waitress a smile before she slipped through the curtain.

As she sat with Levi, Rhi's mind went blank. Her throat grew drier and drier the longer they sat there. Her breath caught. Good Lord, how many first dates had she been on? This shouldn't be this hard. She cleared her throat, grabbed her drink, and took a sip. The cold liquid lodged in her throat, and she barely had time to grab a napkin before she coughed some of it up.

"Are you okay?" Levi handed her another napkin.

She took it, cleared her throat a few times, and finally caught her breath enough to speak. "Tell me what you like to do in your spare time?"

Levi quirked a brow at her. "You okay?"

"Well, I had to break the tension somehow...I was choking on it."

"You choked on wine—not tension." He winked at her. "And why is there tension? We do this on a regular basis."

"Just without the possibility of it going anywhere." She snuggled in closer to him.

"And that makes a difference because? Talk to me. What would we be talking about if this wasn't a first date?"

"What do we want to do the rest of the week?" She smiled. *He's right. No reason to stress about this.*

"Tell me what you want to do. I was hoping we could do some jet skiing. Maybe some island hopping?"

"Yes! I want to go over to the bird sanctuary on the next island over. Oh, and there's the cove. It's my favorite spot here and I don't think I've ever shown you." Rhi took his hand. "When I was a teenager, I'd disappear there to get away from the crazy family."

"While I was out causing trouble with the twins." He chuckled. "I wouldn't mind checking out the farm to see all the upgrades Link's done."

"Right! And Liam's always been up on the latest and greatest entertainment. We can head over to the resort tomorrow and see what he has planned."

"Check out the music scene. I think I remember seeing something about a movie on the beach?"

"I'd rather do something at our own beach. Less people to run into."

"Less people seems to lead to more kissing." He caressed her cheek.

"Kind of thinking that sounds like a good idea. I happen to like kissing you."

He leaned in, his lips inches from hers. "Me too."

The waitress cleared her throat as she set their plates in front of them. "I hope you enjoy the food as much as you seem to be enjoying each other's company." She gave a slight bow and disappeared as quietly as she'd appeared.

"Let's do something private after this."

"Skinny dipping on the private beach?"

"I believe your words earlier were 'why? we have suits.'" Her body heated as an image of the two of them came to her mind.

"I've changed my mind," Levi whispered.

Rhi couldn't help the smile that spread across her face. She bumped his shoulder with her own. "Then I guess we should eat quickly."

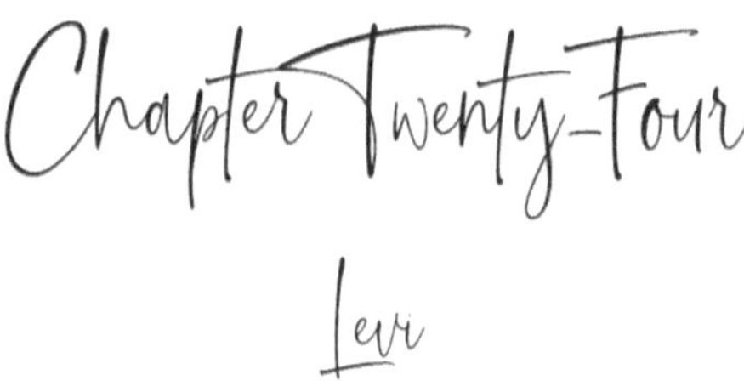

JUNE 9TH

Levi held Rhi's hand as they stood staring out over the sea as the waves gently washed on the shore. "It's a beautiful night."

"The company's nice too." She frowned. "It's super shallow here. You can walk out a hundred feet or more before it goes above our knees."

"Trying to talk me out of the skinny dipping?" He grinned at her.

"I mean, if you want to get naked within eyesight of my mother, you go right ahead."

Levi's eyes crinkled at the corners. "No thank you. What about the pool? You still up for a swim?"

"That sounds perfect." She squeezed his hand as they turned back to the pool.

"You want to do the island-hopping thing tomorrow morning? We can go check out that bird sanctuary, and I'll let you drag me shopping." He teased, but shopping with Rhi was never terrible. She was in and out of most places in a snap. If there were antiques, though, she could get lost for hours.

"Works for me. I'd like to take you to the cove when we get back. It's rather secluded and not too many people know about it."

"Secluded cove with my new girlfriend. Are you trying to seduce me, Miss Edgerly?" He dropped her shoes on one of the chairs next to the pool and faced her.

She wrapped her arms around his neck. "Seduction won't be necessary tomorrow. I plan on doing all my seducing tonight." She kissed his lips then laid a single kiss in the dip of his throat near his Adam's apple.

He groaned. "Not fair...you know all my spots already."

"It *is* fair because you know all of mine too."

Levi spun her so her back was facing him. If she was going to play dirty, so was he. He played his fingers over the muscles of her neck. Gently massaging until she moaned. His lips and tongue followed the same path his fingers just had.

Her legs buckled, and she clutched his shoulder.

He wrapped his other arm around her waist, rubbing circles through her dress above her hip bone.

She moaned. "You're right. This isn't fair."

"You want me to stop?" He nipped her earlobe.

"No." Her voice was no more than a breathless whisper.

"Too bad." He left her on one of the lawn chairs and stripped down to his boxer briefs.

Rhi sat there staring at him. "What are you doing? And why did you stop?"

"I seem to remember plans of swimming."

"Yeah, but that was before..." Rhi stopped and pulled

her dress over her head, revealing a teal strapless bikini that tied in the front. She tossed her dress on the chair.

Levi's gaze swept over her body. "Nice."

"But you haven't been nice." Rhi strode over to him and placed her hands on his chest.

Levi smiled. "Never." He caught her hands as she shoved him backward, pulling her into the water with him.

They both came up sputtering. "What was that for?" Rhi laughed, brushing her hair out of her face.

"Because you *weren't* about to push me in?" Levi pulled her to him.

"Well, of course I was, but you weren't supposed to pull me in too." She pushed him back. "No, you don't get to make my knees go weak again."

"Weren't you supposed to be seducing me?" He dove under the water, swam to the other end of the pool and back, coming up behind her to embrace her again.

The thin fabric of his underwear did nothing to hide his erection pressing against her back. He wanted her more than anyone before. And there was no doubt in his mind he wanted more than a one-night stand.

His lips came down on the back of her neck again, and she tilted her head to give him better access. His hand grazed across her ribs, grabbed the tie on her bikini top, and undid it with one tug.

She gasped, and her hands flew to her chest. "Levi!" She turned around, one hand covering her breasts and the other grasping for her top.

"What?" He threw the top on the deck as he backed her

against the pool wall. "You were the one who suggested skinny dipping."

"Yeah, but we also didn't want to do it in view of my parents."

Even in the pale moonlight, he could see her skin flush. Her lips begged to be kissed.

She folded her arms over her chest to cover herself.

Levi brushed her wet hair away from her face with one hand and touched her arm with the other. "Let me see you. There's no reason to hide from me."

"I…I thought we were waiting?"

"Do you want to?" He took a step away from her. The last thing he wanted to do was stop, but he would.

"N-no." She reached out and pulled him back toward her, still covering her breasts.

Levi drew her into a hug and kissed her forehead. No matter how much he wanted her, he wouldn't do it if there was even the slightest bit of fear.

He reached behind her to grab her top off the deck. "Do you want help putting this on?"

"No, I want you."

"You're scared about something. I can see it in your eyes."

"Please, Levi. I want you. Seriously."

He hugged her tight. "Not tonight."

She took her top from him and turned around to put it back on. "Why are you doing this?"

"Because I know you well enough to know when you're scared, and the last thing I want is for you to regret making love to me."

"The last thing I'm going to do is regret this."

"Good then you'll have a negative amount of regret if we wait."

Rhi turned toward him and snorted. "Negative regret?"

He shrugged. "All the blood in my body is in the wrong head to be coming up with something clever."

She secured her bikini top and groaned. "You're stopping? No chance I could get your motor running again?" She ran her fingers down his chest.

"The motor never stopped running, but we're not going there tonight." He hopped up onto the deck and reached down to help her out. "We should have brought towels."

"I shouldn't have been hesitant." Rhi picked up her dress and shoes from the chair.

"You can't help how you feel. And I don't want *any* fear when we do go there." He gathered his own clothes and offered her his hand. "Would you like me to stay with you? After my cold shower?"

Rhi's face brightened. "I knew you wouldn't give up that easily."

"Not giving up at all. Just making sure you're ready." He caressed her cheek. "And I don't care how many cold showers I have to take. It's not happening tonight." He kissed her lips—a single peck—then pulled away, put his arm around her, and led her back to their cabin.

Chapter Twenty-Five

Rhi

JUNE 10TH

Rhi sat in the living area in the main pavilion, waiting for Levi.

Her mom came in and joined her on the couch. "What are your plans for the evening?"

"I want to take Levi to the cove while we're still here, but it's hard to get to in the dark." She rested her elbows on her knees and her chin on her hands.

"You're disappointed." Her mother rubbed her back. "Tell him."

"It's not that. We can go tomorrow. I messed up last night. We were getting pretty hot and heavy, and I guess I looked scared or something, so he stopped."

"Most women would find that endearing. He didn't make you continue even though you were unsure. He put your needs before his own."

Rhi let out a deep breath. Her mother was right, no matter how much she didn't want to admit it. How many times had she wished for a guy who did what Levi did? "I didn't want him to stop."

"There will be other times. Seduce him. Make sure he knows you want him as much as he wants you."

"But what if he sees the same look on my face like he did last night?"

"You're telling me there was no doubt in your mind last night about taking the next step with your best friend. You weren't scared sex could irreversibly change everything between you two?"

"Okay, maybe there was a little fear. But I don't think that's going to change until after it happens."

"Then talk to him about it. He needs to know how you're feeling."

Rhi hugged her mother. "I hate that you're right."

Jen grinned. "I've seen the in-love-with-my-best-friend thing play out before." She hugged her daughter back.

The door opened, and Levi inched through. "How embarrassing would this conversation have been for me?" He came around the couch and kissed both women on the cheeks.

"Why do you think we're talking about you?" Jen winked.

"Don't you always?"

Rhi snorted. "Not always, but we were this time."

"I may have lost my sleazeball card last night, but it was only a matter of time." He grinned and plopped into the armchair.

"I don't think you've ever had a sleazeball card." Jen patted him on the back.

"I can name quite a few women who'd disagree with you."

"That's because they didn't take you seriously when you said you didn't do more than one-night stands." Rhi scowled and crossed her arms over her chest. She didn't want to think of him with other women.

"Hey, I know we talked about going to the cove, but I figured we could go over to the resort instead since it's getting late. They're showing all three of the original Star Wars movies on the beach."

Rhi frowned. "I know it's my favorite to binge, but I thought we didn't want to be around a bunch of people."

"It's a private island, Rhi." Jen chuckled.

Levi nodded. "She has a point. And I can't see there being a ton of Star Wars nerds here."

"Lex and Chelsea will be there."

"So? We'll tease them about making out then do it ourselves." Levi laughed. "Come on...I know how much you love the movies. I'll be the Han to your Leia. Tell me you love me."

"I do love you."

He stood and did his best Harrison Ford impression. "I know."

"And you're an ass."

"I know that too." He grasped her hands, pulled her to her feet, and gave her a quick kiss. "Come on, nerd queen. Let's go be extra nerdy."

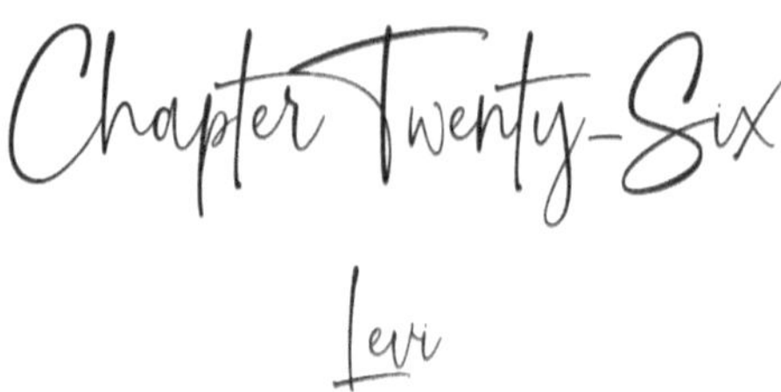

June 13th

L evi stared into the refrigerator and groaned. He wasn't even hungry. Well, not for food, at least. He slammed the door shut and raked a hand through his hair.

"Hey, you have time to sign some papers for me?" Leon strolled to the table and grabbed a stack of papers.

"Sure." He sat down, welcoming the distraction.

Leon put down two stacks of paper in front of him. "I wasn't sure how you'd want to do this. The first bundle is full ownership—lock, stock, and barrel. The second is co-ownership between the two of us for the first two years, then it all goes to you."

"I'm good with co-ownership for the first two years. I'd like the extra cushion in case anything happens I'm not ready for."

"Oh, it will. Believe me…it will. I've been in business long enough to know there will be pitfalls."

"Hell, I've seen it too many times just working for someone else." He picked up the pen and signed the paper in front of him to become a partner.

"I'm okay if you want to take full ownership now or any time in the next two years. I'll give it over willingly. I want you to succeed. And to let you know now, our network administrator is thinking about retiring, so you'll need a new one pretty soon."

"I appreciate that, but I think the partnership will be a better idea. Besides, I'm twenty-four. You could grow to hate me in the next two years." *What if I break Rhi's heart? What if something happens and none of them want to see me again?* He pushed his thoughts aside, signed the papers, and stood up.

"Something bothering you?"

"Yeah. But it's nothing I can talk to my girlfriend's father about."

"We're all open around here. Jen gave you the sex talk." Leon chuckled.

"Yeah. More than once, much to my dismay." Levi smiled at Leon. "I just need a little time to myself."

"Have fun."

Levi rushed out of the room. He should be happy. He'd just signed paperwork to take over a well-established company. His head spun. Would her dad take it all away from him if they didn't work out? He made it to the door just as Rhi came in.

She smiled at him. "Hey, you. Want to go over to the cove? We're leaving tomorrow and I'd like to show it to you."

"Give me an hour, please?" He kissed her cheek. He hated to disappoint her, but he needed some time. The last thing he wanted to do was break it off because of the thoughts racing through his head.

Her smile faded, but she nodded. "Take all the time you need."

"Rhi." He lifted her chin. "I'm not putting you off, I promise. We'll go tonight."

"It's a bit of a hike and hard to get to when it's dark." She let out a sigh and turned away from him.

"I promise."

She disappeared into the other room.

Damn. He raked a hand through his hair and blew out a breath as he walked outside.

It took him five minutes to get to the farm. He knocked on Link's door.

Link smiled as he opened the door. "Hey, man, what's up?"

"I just signed a contract with Rhi's dad to take over his company in two years. What happens if this doesn't work out with Rhi? What if I break her heart?" He hurried inside and paced across the living room.

"Whoa. Our family knew you long before you and Rhi became an item. They've accepted you as one of them." Link went into the kitchen and returned with two bottles of water. He tossed one to Levi.

"Leon's not going to want to work with me if I break his daughter's heart. Not to mention the fact she's mad at me right now."

"Why?"

"I've been trying to be good. I've avoided being alone with her for more than an hour or two at a time. But, damn, it's getting hard."

"Are you sick? Dude you've slept with half the employees on the island."

Levi sent him a glare. "It was one."

"Not that I want to hear about my cousin's sex life, but why are you waiting? It's not like she's a wait until marriage kind of gal."

"I want us both to be sure." Levi dropped onto the couch. "Our friendship has changed, but this is the last line to cross. This could ruin any possibility of going back."

Link shrugged. "Or you two could find out you're perfect for each other, which all of us have been saying for years by the way."

"I know, I just…maybe I'm a little scared."

"Aren't we all." Link smiled at him. "Speaking of Rhi, I wanted to ask you if she's happy with her job?"

"Recently, not so much, why?"

"Our social media director bailed on us two days ago. Took a bunch of money allocated for a big project he was supposed to be doing and disappeared. Dad wanted me to see if she'd be interested in the position, even temporarily or part time just to get us through until we could hire someone else, or she had time to go full time."

Levi shrugged. "Ask her. I'm sure she'd be willing to help out."

"Thanks, man. I'll talk to her tomorrow before you all leave."

Levi snapped his fingers. "Tell me about the cove?"

"Rhi's favorite spot? It's on the other side of the island. There's a bit of rough terrain on the way in. You can't swim 'cause of the rocks, but there's a nice, secluded shore there."

"Could we have a romantic dinner and camp out there?"

"Hell ya! We could set that up for you. Give me half an hour." Link pulled out his phone and sent a text message. "Go see her. Everything will be ready by the time you get there."

Levi took a deep breath. If everything went well, they'd know exactly where their relationship stood. "All right. Half an hour. We'll be there."

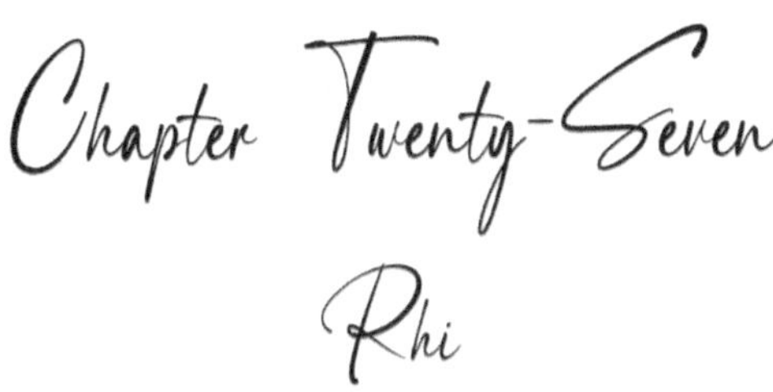

Chapter Twenty-Seven

Rhi

Rhi threw herself onto her bed and screamed into her pillow. If Levi broke his promise, she was going to call it all off. All she wanted to do was take the man she loved to her favorite spot on the island.

The man she loved. The words echoed in her head. How many times had she told Levi she loved him before? She didn't want to break it off with him. She wanted him to talk to her and spend time with her like they always did. Dating shouldn't make that any different.

The door to their cabin opened, and she glanced toward her entryway. *Please don't stand me up.* She buried her head in her pillow again, not wanting him to see her upset.

The bed sank next to her, and Levi's scent surrounded her. He pulled her into a tight embrace. "Don't be mad at me."

She rolled over and rested her head on his chest. "I'm not mad. I just wanted to show you the cove. It's my favorite place."

"Then take me." Levi lifted her chin and pressed a kiss

to her lips. "I'm done avoiding things. I want this to work out."

"Me too. I don't want to be scared we'll ruin our friendship. I want to know we'll be closer."

"I think we're doing that. There would have been several freeze moments if we weren't more open with each other."

"I didn't even think about that. I knew you'd come talk to me eventually." She sat up on the bed. "Will you let me take you to the cove?"

"You bet. But grab extra clothes. I was thinking maybe we'd camp out there." He sat up next to her.

"Since when do we camp?" She snickered. The only time they ever camped was when they were kids. And one time, they'd slept in the back of his SUV when they got caught in a snowstorm.

"Just bring clothes. If you don't want to do it when we get there we can always come back." Levi kissed her cheek and headed into his room.

Rhi went to her suitcase. She'd need real shoes for the hike, but she could wear flip-flops when they arrived. Camping at the cove. Maybe she could convince him she was ready.

She put on the teal bathing suit she'd worn the other night then her short blue jean shorts and a teal halter over the top. Extra clothes and shoes went into a bag, along with some toiletries she wasn't sure she'd use.

She slung the bag over her shoulder and walked into Levi's room. "Ready."

He glanced at his watch. "How long does it take to walk there?"

"Maybe twenty minutes from here. We can take the main road for most of it."

"Think you're up for the hike?"

"Always. With as much good food as we've eaten the last couple days, I need the exercise." She laughed.

"Good." Levi took her bag and slipped it into his own. "Let's go." He put his arm around her, and they trekked out of their cabin.

Companionable silence accompanied them on their walk. They held hands most of the way, smiling at each other when they caught the other looking.

Rhi tugged on his hand when she saw the path leading toward the cove. The terrain wasn't terrible, but there were rocks they had to climb over.

She stopped when the rocks grew taller and the walls around them became closer together. "Are you ready to see my favorite place in the world?"

"You bet. Lead me in."

She took his hand and led him down the path. When the beach appeared before them, her eyes went wide.

A large tent was adorned with white twinkle lights, a full-size mattress, blankets, and pillows. The table was fully set, and a cooler sat next to it.

She turned around to stare at him. "How did you do this?"

"I wish I could take the credit. I asked Link about the cove and wondered if we could camp here. He took care of the rest."

"It's even more amazing than it was before. She pushed up on her toes and pressed a kiss to his lips. "Thank you."

"Dinner first or should we check out the bed?"

"Are we going to go there?"

"Well, I figured we'd talk through our concerns first, but I'm not going to deny wanting you, Rhi." He ran his fingers down her spine, cupped her behind, and pulled her against him.

"I want you too." Her body shivered as she pressed a kiss to his throat.

Levi picked her up and carried her to the bed. He laid her down and joined her, kicking off his shoes as he did.

Rhi removed her shoes and socks and rolled over so she was facing him. "Do you have concerns?"

"I want our friendship—and our relationship—to get stronger with this. I don't want it to end."

"It won't ever be the same but a different level of intimacy."

"I'm good with that." He brushed a stray hair out of her face. "I had a moment earlier after I signed the paperwork to take over your father's business. I'm going to be a partner for the next two years. And I couldn't get past the thought of this not ending well. What if this ruins our friendship and I break your heart? That's why I left so quickly. I didn't want to end any possibility we had together because of a moment of fear."

"We could have talked through it."

"We are now. But I needed space."

"I understand. I wasn't mad. I just felt like you were avoiding me all day. And it's our last night here and I really wanted to show you this place."

"I'm glad I let you. Maybe we can make it a Rhi and Levi only place."

"Well, my family does own the island. We could probably make it off limits." She chuckled.

Levi caressed her face. "I want you, but if you have *any* hesitation about this, I need to know."

"I don't. I want you too." She kissed his neck, sliding her hands down his white T-shirt.

Levi grabbed her hand and brought it to his lips, kissing her inner wrist at the pulse point.

Rhi kissed his fingers as they traced the outline of her lips. She opened her lips and nipped at his fingertip.

He moaned and crushed his lips to hers. He wrapped his arm around her and ran his fingernails slowly down the back of her neck.

She gasped, clutched his arms, and thrust her tongue between his lips, quickly losing her ability to think. Every touch made her want him more and more.

Levi pulled his lips away from hers, pressing soft kisses on her neck. He nipped and kissed behind her ears. His hands went down and caught the bottom of her shirt, pulling away long enough to yank it over her head and toss it to the ground.

She whispered his name against his neck as he unhooked her bra, removing it and throwing it on the ground next to them. The cool ocean breeze blew through the tent, and her hard nipples tightened further.

He lowered her to her back, straddling her thighs. His lips returned to her body and moved across her collarbone, down her neck, and lower to her breasts. He traced his tongue in circles around her nipples, and his fingers brushed them with light strokes, pinching one while sucking the other.

Rhi's hips bucked against him as her sex heated to burning. "Levi, please." She wanted to feel him inside her. To have him touch her there for the first time.

"Please what?" He suckled on her nipple again, his hand gliding down toward her sex.

"Yesss." She caught his hand and guided it down until it hovered over her. "Please. Touch me."

"I am." His lips followed the same path his hand did. He kissed her stomach and traced her belly button with her tongue.

Rhi squeezed her hips together. She ached...burned. Every kiss, every caress with his tongue was torture as she waited breathlessly for him to touch her most intimate part.

He reached the waistband of her jeans and unbuttoned them.

She rushed to lower her zipper and push her shorts off.

Levi took over, stripping her bare, spread out on the bed before him.

She pressed her hips forward, begging for his touch, her eyes closed as she waited. "Levi."

He lowered his head again, pushing her legs apart as his lips came down on her inner thighs. Her body trembled as he licked and kissed his way closer and closer to her sex.

Her hips came off the bed when his lips finally touched her clit.

He suckled, lapping his tongue over it in short steady movements. He entered her with one finger, curling it in a come-hither motion, pushing her over the edge when he touched her g-spot.

Her fingers dug into his shoulders, and she screamed out his name as the waves of her orgasm washed over her.

He continued his ministrations until her hips stopped pulsing and her fingers relaxed. He moved up her body again and dropped down beside her. He held her tightly as aftershocks ran through her.

"Good for you?" he whispered in her ear.

His breath on her ear made her whole body tingle.

"It's never been like this."

He jumped up and stripped off his T-shirt, shorts, and boxer briefs.

She stared at him for a moment then reached out to touch him.

He batted her hand away. "Not until you answer my question."

"What question?" She frowned. "I didn't even hear you ask one."

"I know." He flashed her favorite grin.

She smacked his shoulder. "Damn it, Levi. You know I hate it when you make me giggle."

"Oh, I'm gonna make you do a lot more than giggle." He laid down next to her and traced his hand over her side. "Now about the question. Did my kiss ever make it past a ten?"

"Really now? You want to know that?"

"Of course." He wrapped his arms around her, rolled onto his back, and pulled her on top of him. "'Cause you well surpassed my wildest dreams."

"How high does the scale actually go? You said one to

ten but said I was between ten and eleven?" She rocked her hips, his erection pushing against her.

He groaned. "You're at *least* an eleven…probably closer to a twelve."

Her chuckle shook her entire body.

Levi let out a long moan. "I don't even care. Just ride me."

Rhi pushed up, wrapped her hand around his cock, and guided him inside her. She moaned as she lowered herself until he was buried deep inside her. She placed her hands on his chest and rocked back and forth. Her eyes closed, and she instinctively moved faster.

Levi grasped her hips, pushing his own up higher. His thumb touched her clit, rubbing slow circles as she rode him.

Her fingernails dug into his chest as her climax built again.

"I can't hold it much longer." Sweat beaded on his brow. His eyes were closed, and his lips parted.

"Don't hold back," she whispered as her own orgasm grew to the point of no return. She cried out as her muscles clenched around him, bringing him to climax, his seed spilling deep inside her. She collapsed on top of him, her energy spent.

Levi wrapped his arms around her, rubbing circles on her back as their heart rates and breathing slowed.

She slid off him and curled up next to him, resting her head on his shoulder. "It's never been like that before."

"Never for me either." He pulled a blanket over them. "Amazing isn't a strong enough word."

"Stupendous? Astounding?"

"Better, but still not quite what I'm looking for." He kissed her forehead and hugged her close. "Perfect would be most accurate."

She smiled. "And our friendship?"

"Intact and even stronger than before?"

She draped her arm across his chest. "Perfect is right, and your kisses are a twelve."

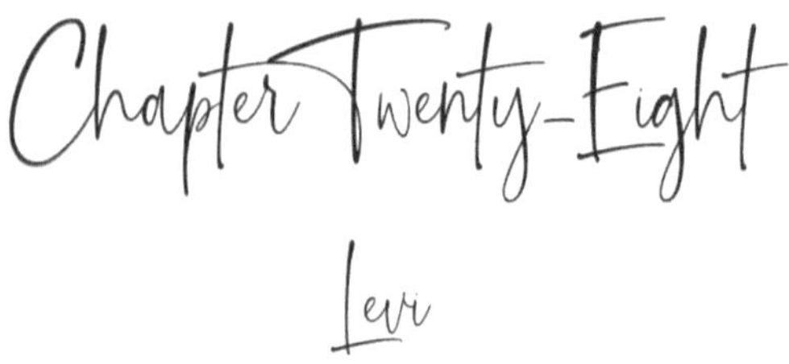

Chapter Twenty-Eight

Levi

A loud squawk brought Levi out of a dead sleep. He scanned the area for the cause of the offending noise.

A large white bird was perched on the rocks across from their tent. It squawked again.

Rhi bolted upright, pulling the sheet over her chest. "What the hell was that?"

Levi pointed to the creature. "I think it's staring at us."

Rhi peaked around him. "That thing's huge."

"That's what—"

"Don't even go there." She shook her finger at him.

The bird let out a third squawk and took to the sky. It circled then landed on the ground closer to them. It took a step forward on its long legs.

"I think it wants to be where we are." Rhi grasped Levi's shoulder. "Where's a cat when you need one?"

"I don't think Duke would mess with that." Levi chuckled then put on his shorts before climbing out of bed.

"Be careful." Rhi bit her lip.

Levi moved out of the tent and inched toward the bird.

The bird turned its head to look at him and took another step near the table.

"I think it's going for the bread." Levi crept over, grabbed one of the rolls, broke it into chunks, and tossed it to the animal.

The bird snatched up the pieces and gobbled them down.

Levi threw the rest of the loaf away from them and moved back to the tent. "It's just hungry."

Rhi's stomach growled. "Me too. We didn't eat last night."

"I'm assuming there's a generator around here since the cooler has a cord coming out of it. And these lights are being run from somewhere. You wanna see what they left us?"

"Sure." Rhi put on the long T-shirt and gave him a quick kiss on the cheek.

He pulled her down onto his lap. "How are you feeling about us this morning?"

She smiled. "Like I want to wake up with you every morning?"

"I'm feeling the same way, preferably without the bird though." He kissed her nose. "Now the question is…whose bed do we sleep in?"

Rhi laughed. "Mine, of course. It's newer and less contaminated than yours."

"Hey, I wash my sheets, thank you very much." Levi tickled her side.

She giggled. "More like *I* wash your sheets. You call me

in there to walk you through the process every time you need to do something."

"Yeah, I just like watching you bend down to pick up stuff."

Rhi smacked him in the arm. "That would imply you wanted me well before we got together."

"Nope, rule number one. No implying anything about the pre-Levi-and-Rhi relationship."

The bird circled again then landed on the table.

Rhi flinched. "Why is it back? There's no more bread."

"Are you seriously afraid of birds?"

"Ones this big that are staring at me, yes! Also, any flying insect besides flies, but you already know this." She climbed out of his lap and hid behind him. "Make it go away. Or I'll tell it about your fear of spiders."

"It's not a fear. It's a healthy reaction to a dangerous creature. And I don't think this bird is going to care. It would probably eat them."

"Healthy reaction, my ass. You screamed when a little one joined you in the shower."

"Keep it up and I'll let the bird have you." Levi climbed off the bed and shooed the bird to get it to go away.

The bird hopped off the table and squawked again.

Rhi pointed to the cooler. "Dump the food. Give it anything it wants."

Levi snorted. "What is this, a hostage situation?"

Rhi glared at him. "If you make me deal with this bird, I will make you deal with every spider in the apartment or any future residence for the rest of eternity."

"That's what exterminators are for." Levi got closer to

the bird and tried shooing it away again. "Go on, get out of here."

The bird moved closer then stuck his beak between Levi and Rhi.

Rhi jumped back. "It's attacking me."

The bird snatched a lone piece of bread from the ground then took flight away from the camp.

"It attacked you *so* bad. Are you sure you'll make it back all right?"

"My boss raises tarantulas. I may have her bring them over to show you." She took a step toward him.

Levi reached out and pulled her close. "Oh yeah? Well I think our next pet should be a parrot."

Rhi curled her hands around his neck. "There was a spider with a giant egg sack right outside our building. I wonder how many babies I could hatch in the apartment."

He lifted her off her feet. "Rule number two. I will refrain from bringing birds in the house as long as Rhi refrains from bringing spiders."

"Deal. Now shut up and kiss me."

The chime of Rhi's phone stopped him from kissing her right away. She growled, wriggled out of his grasp, and hurried over to check her phone. "It's my boss."

"It's Saturday. Doesn't she ever take time off?" Levi dropped down on the bed and slipped his arm around her.

"She does." Rhi read the text and grimaced. "She wants me back in the office on Monday."

Levi shrugged. "We can look for houses another day this week or even this coming weekend. No big deal."

Rhi shook her head. "Yeah, it is. I took my vacation

time the way I did for a reason." She shot her boss a quick text and turned back to Levi, groaning the second her phone started ringing. She hit the answer button and put it on speaker. "Hello, Delilah."

"I need you back Monday. This can't wait until Tuesday. This social media calendar can't wait any longer. It's waited too long for you to get done with your blasted vacation. I need you in the office every day to make sure these are posted and answered as soon as possible."

"I told you before I left, I'm looking at houses in Bryton when I get back and I might not always be able to be in the office." Rhi glanced over at Levi, who shrugged.

"Are you still on this whole moving with your best friend thing? What about your job? You can't just up and move with your friend and have no job to fall back on. That makes no sense at all."

"He's not just my best friend now, Delilah." Rhi reached out and took Levi's hand. "We're dating now."

"Right. The two best friends who never wanted anything more than friendship are now dating. You think I'm that gullible?"

"Whatever you want to believe, I'm telling you now that I'm not going to be in the office everyday anymore. We talked about this, and I thought you were okay with it."

"Well, I'm not. And if you can't commit to this company, maybe you need to find another job." Delilah hung up the phone.

Rhi's jaw dropped. "Did she just fire me?"

"Kinda sounds like she did." Levi laid back on the pillows. "Come lay with me. We'll talk about it."

Rhi stared at her phone before lying down next to Levi. "I've never been fired."

"At least if she fired you, you can draw unemployment and still have money coming in while you're looking for something."

"I know, but I don't know how much unemployment is. I've never even thought about that."

"Sixty percent of your base annual income, if I remember right." Levi ran his hand down her arm. "You'll do fine on that."

"But we're moving."

"Like I said, you have money. We don't have to worry about this. Not to mention the fact that I'm partnering with your dad and pretty much running the company. I have expensive taste but not enough to spend a ton on a place to live." Levi pulled her into his arms. "It will be all right. I don't mind taking care of the bills while you look for something."

"But I've always picked up my share, even if we split it month-by-month."

"We've also never been in a relationship before." Levi brushed her hair out of her face. "It wouldn't have mattered if we were just friends or not. If you'd lost your job or were looking for another, I wouldn't have a problem helping out."

"You don't understand. I don't like not being able to pull my own weight."

"Shit, I forgot to tell you. Link mentioned something yesterday about a part-time position in social media. They're looking for someone to take over on a temporary basis until they find someone to replace the guy that just screwed them over."

"That would be great, but it's not going to work if I have to stay here."

"You'll have to talk to him about the details, but if you could do it from home, it would be a great way to supplement your income."

Rhi took a deep breath. "It would make it so I wasn't worthless."

"You'll never be worthless to me no matter how much money you did or didn't bring in. Besides, if you're not there, who's going to have dinner on the table for me every night?"

Rhi laughed. "Right, we'll be in Bryton. Where do you think we're going to eat most nights?"

"Mom's, takeout, occasionally Dad will torture food for us?" Levi chuckled.

"Exactly. We're both culinarily challenged."

"I wouldn't say *challenged*. We both like to eat and know good food. Domestically challenged would be more correct. Remember when you put a red shirt in with all my whites?"

"I fixed that before they went in the dryer. I'm thankful for whoever created color catchers." Rhi smirked. "And who broke the dishwasher overloading it?"

"I swear that was Robby. I had it full and everything was all nice and neat, then he went through and added a bunch more shit."

"Sure, it was."

"Dude, I know how to load the dishwasher. Grandma

Edgerly drilled it in my head because I put them in wrong the one time when I was ten."

Rhi snuggled in closer to him. "We should have done this a long time ago."

"Nothing wrong with not recognizing it right away. Sometimes you just need extra time to get things right." Levi traced his fingers between her hip and her knee.

"Keep doing that and we're not going to get back on time."

He glanced at his watch. "We have exactly two hours until we need to start packing up. That gives us plenty of time to get lost in each other at least one more time."

"If that's the case, shut up and kiss me."

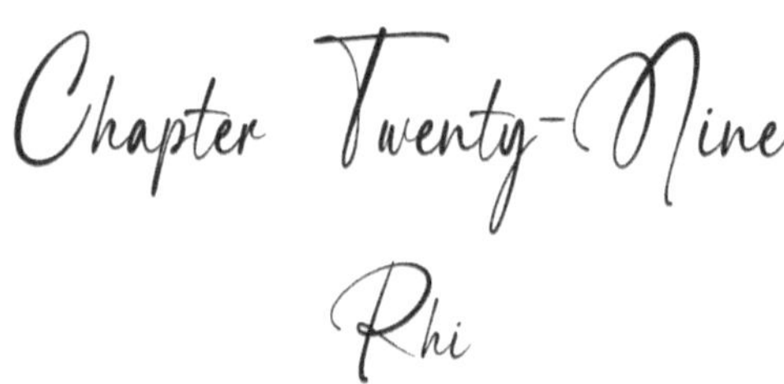

Chapter Twenty-Nine

Rhi

Rhi sighed as she packed up her things. She wasn't ready to go home. Would she and Levi fall back into the routine of just friends?

His arms snaked around her waist and his lips touched her neck. "I don't want to leave paradise."

"Me neither." She groaned. "Better stop now or we'll be late for the boat."

"Yeah, right. Your mom will be in here forcing us out of this room in five minutes."

"I know. I've been waiting for her to come in for a while." Rhi turned and hugged Levi. "We're not going back to being friends, right?"

"No way." He squeezed her. "It's you and me now."

The door opened. "Okay, you two. I need you ready to go in two minutes," Jen called from the other room.

"I'm surprised she didn't barge in. We should get naked in case she does." Levi winked at her.

Rhi laughed. "Almost ready, Mom."

"Good. Then get out here so I can do the final missing item inspection."

Rhi pulled away from Levi and zipped her suitcase. "Ready?"

"As I'll ever be." Levi gripped the handles of their suitcases and moved into the other room.

Rhi threw her overnight bag over her shoulder and followed him.

Her mom smiled at both of them. "You have no idea how excited I am that you two are together."

"You've told us a thousand times, Mom." Rhi rolled her eyes.

"Well, I figured since it took you so long to get together, you might need a couple reminders. Time for the final sweep." Jen shuffled through the other rooms checking for stray items.

"Didn't you do that?"

"Of course I did. I've been through every room three times this morning. Where do you think I got it from?"

"You're gonna do that when we move from our condo in Indy?" Levi put his arm around.

"Do you not remember when we moved out of the apartments on campus? Auntie Jackie did the final inspection like she does with her real estate clients."

"I remember."

Jen stepped out of the last room. "All clear. Rhi, I think you have this clearing out a hotel room thing figured out."

"I learned from the best." She smiled at her mom and gave her a hug. Jen could be a handful sometimes, but she admired her. "I love you, Mom."

"I love you too, honey. Now let's head for the docks. We don't want to be late."

"Like they'd leave without us. We're family." Levi put up his hands.

"Well, Link and Liam are piloting today, so you never can tell with those boys." Jen grinned. "Let's go."

The ride to the docks was chaos. Kym was convinced she left something in her room, despite her and Jen checking three times. Chelsea and Lex hid in the back, whispering to each other.

Rhi leaned into Levi. "It's times like these I remember why I'm glad I moved in with you right after college."

"I mean, I'm only one person, but I think I stir up some drama now and then. Watch this." He climbed off the cart. "Hey, Kym, did you look behind the nightstand?"

Her eyes went wide. "No, I didn't. Mom, we have to go back and check."

Jen glared at Levi. "You may not be blood, but when you were five, your father gave me full permission to spank you, and don't think I won't take advantage of that now."

"I can go further. You know what Lex and Chelsea have been talking about?" Levi grinned.

Rhi clapped her hands over his mouth. "We just started dating and I'd like you to live past this trip."

Levi licked her hand and she pulled it away. "I mean, you just told me how much you miss your family in times like this. So I had to up the ante."

"Go get in the boat before Jen beats you." Leon smiled and pushed them forward.

Rhi took Levi's hand, and they walked onto the dock.

Liam greeted them as they climbed aboard. "I saw the look Aunt Jen gave you. Are you messing up again?"

Levi laughed. "I may have freaked Kym out a bit and now she wants to go back to the house to do another sweep for anything left behind."

"Teenage siblings are the best to mess with." Liam snickered. "How's the Social Media Queen today?"

"Sad we're going home. Levi said you talked to him about a job for me?"

"Our last social media director ran off with a bunch of money, so we're out both the money and the director. Dad's not sure what he wants to do as far as a full-time thing, but he's looking for someone temporary for now. Interested?"

"Let me get back home and see what I can work out. I think I was just fired. If that's true, I'd love to help. How much time would I be expected to be on the island?" Rhi smiled at him.

"We have a photographer on site, and Liam and I can send you all the information about upcoming events and stuff like that. I don't see why you couldn't do it from home."

"Now I wish Delilah had been more clear."

Levi took her phone.

"What are you doing?" Rhi quirked her brows at him.

"Finding out if you're fired." He tapped on the screen a few times then handed the phone back.

"What?!" She stared down, waiting for a text to come through. "At least let Uncle Len know I'm interested. If it's part time, even if I still have a job, I'm sure I could work it into my schedule."

"I'll tell him later today and have him send you the details, but I guarantee the pay is good."

"Nice. I'll wait for his message." Rhi stepped aside so others could board the boat.

Levi put his arm around her and walked toward the ship's bow. "You should quit and take the offer."

"I definitely want it, but if she didn't fire me, I don't want to leave her in a bind."

"From what I heard, she's firing you if you're not in the office Monday morning."

"I don't think I *can* be in the office then. We're not going to be back until tomorrow, and I wasn't even planning on us leaving Bryton until Monday. There's no reason to rush home if we plan on spending the following day there."

"Right. I guess we wait to see what she has to say."

Her phone chimed, and she read the message from Delilah.

DELILAH:

You're fired. Is that clear enough? Your
stuff will be in a box whenever you decide
to grace us with your presence.

"That was fast. It's official. I've been fired." Rhi held up her phone to show Levi.

"Good. Go tell Link you want the job." Levi chuckled. "We'll stay in Bryton until we find a place then head back to Indy to start packing things up."

Rhi bit her lip then let a smile grow. "This feels like the start of something good."

"You bet it is."

Rhi leaned into Levi's chest. "I want every day to be like this."

"I don't want to live on the water. And considering I just signed a contract with your dad, I'm not sure staying here would be the best idea."

She glared at him. "You and me...together like this. Not necessarily on this boat."

"Well, that we can arrange." Levi hugged her close. "I want us to be together as well."

Chapter Thirty

Rhi

JUNE 16TH

Rhi rubbed the back of her neck then climbed into the car. "I'm not sold on any of the apartments so far."

"Jackie said there's condos, townhouses, and duplexes we could look at as well." Levi reached over and squeezed her hand. "We don't have to decide anything today."

"I know. I'm being picky. The ones on the lake weren't too bad."

"We're not settling for something that's 'not too bad.' We'll find something you love, even if it takes a bit."

There was a knock on the window.

Levi opened the door to talk to Jackie. "Where to next?"

"I know you're not sold on the idea of houses, but there are two cute ones down the street. They're relatively new, so there shouldn't be much updating and they're still on the small side."

Levi glanced over at Rhi. "What do you think?"

"Can't be any worse than the ones we've already looked at."

"You're right about that, dear. I need to re-evaluate some of my rental listings. Those places need some major updates." Jackie typed something into her phone and smiled. "Follow me down the road."

Levi shut the door and started the car. "Ready?"

"I guess." Rhi stared out the window.

"What do you think about a house?"

"How different is it going to be? We've always been in apartments or condos. A house feels like a big commitment."

"I mean, we can check out the condos or townhouses instead?"

"I was thinking about the logistics. Owning a house means fixing your own problems. Renting would come with landlords for that."

"There's nothing to stop us from hiring someone to do maintenance for us. And we'd have more control over what we could do. You could even paint a wall peach like you always wanted to do here."

"And as owners, there'd be no one to complain when I put holes in the wall while hanging pictures."

Levi snorted. "Yeah, you should probably leave that to me. I'm a little more handy than you."

"Who fixed the washer? Or the fridge?"

"Menards fixed the fridge. We bought a new one. And it was you who didn't remember to take things out of their pocket that broke the dryer in the first place." Levi smiled.

"Milo gave me a rock. I didn't remember I put it in my pocket until I pulled it out of the dryer."

Levi followed her aunt into the driveway of a small yellow house. "House, condo, or apartment?"

"I feel like I'm playing the game kids Edge's age used to play. What was it? MASH? Mansion, apartment, shack, or house? Should we draw until someone says stop so I can count the lines?"

"Speaking of Edge, he offered you his house."

"What?"

"The night we went out on the island and Sara was helping you get ready?"

"Yeah?"

"He and I talked for a while, and he said that if you want the house, he'd give it to you."

"Like free and clear? No money changes hands?"

"That's what it sounded like to me."

"That's a big house. What would we do with all that space?"

"I don't know. I just forgot to tell you before now."

"Let's at least look at the other houses. I'll think about Edge's house too."

"Good plan." Levi climbed out of the car, came around the side, and opened the door for her. "I kinda like the color and it doesn't look that much bigger than our apartment."

"Does it have a garage? An attached one would be preferable. If we're getting a house, I don't want to have to wade through the snow to bring in groceries."

"You have groceries delivered. We don't even have to leave the house." Levi winked.

Jackie walked over to them. "There's an attached two-car garage behind the house. It's fully insulated and heated, so you'll be plenty warm."

"That would lead to having the driveway plowed in the snow." Rhi grimaced. "Houses sound expensive."

"There's a lot of money saved with owning a house, dear, especially if you buy outright. Yes, you do need to pay for maintenance and upkeep, but how much are you paying now in rent?"

Rhi looked at Levi. "What, like three grand a month?"

Levi nodded. "That includes utilities though."

"You get double the space and still wouldn't pay more than five hundred a month in utilities." Jackie punched in the code on the key box then unlocked the door.

"Plus, we could put some of our former rent money aside to pay for repairs." Levi glanced around the front room. "It seems smart to me."

Rhi turned and put her hand on his head. "No fever. Are you sure you're *actually* Levi? Because my Levi doesn't do commitments."

Levi put his arms around her. "That changed when I woke up and realized the perfect woman was with me all along."

"You mean all those girls who told you they were the right one?" Rhi cocked her head and gave him a wink.

"Yep, but I already had the right girl. I just wasn't looking at her with a clear head."

Rhi laughed. "Come on, let's take the grand tour."

Twenty minutes later, Jackie led them into the living room. "What do you think? Still small enough that the upkeep wouldn't be bad."

"It doesn't feel much bigger than our apartment." Rhi

glanced over her shoulder at the hallway that led to the two other bedrooms.

Levi frowned. "I don't know, there's some upgrades that would need to be done. It doesn't feel as modern as I'd like."

"If you want modern, I have just the place for you." Jackie moved to the door and motioned them to follow her. "Two doors down, recently built. It's a little larger and a little pricier, but I think you'll love it."

Rhi took a deep breath and caught Levi's arm as he went to follow Jackie. "Can you give us a few, Aunt Jackie?"

"Of course, dear. Take all the time you want. We can leave your car here and drive over there together." She breezed out of the house.

Levi wrapped his arms around Rhi. "Trying to get me alone so we can sneak off into the other room?"

Rhi broke out of his grasp and stepped away. "Is this what we want? What happens if we don't work out? Are you sure we want to buy a house together after we just started dating?"

Levi took her hand. "We've lived together for the last five years. Other than sharing a bed now, how is this going to be any different?"

"We're in love now, but what if that changes? If we split the cost of buying this place and break up, we're both stuck with a mortgage to a house that one of us might not even be living in." Rhi squeezed his hand. "I don't want to end up regretting doing this."

"Then we go back to looking at apartments." Levi

dropped her hand. "I'll let Jackie know we're done for the day." He strode to the door.

"Levi, wait." Rhi hurried and stopped in front of him. "This is a big decision."

"One that should be thought about overnight instead of jumped into head first?" He moved around her and out the door.

Rhi blew out a breath. She followed him, closing and locking the door behind her.

Jackie met her on the porch. "Levi said you're done for the day?"

Rhi shook her head. "Let's go see the other house. I don't want to end this day on a bad note."

"You two fighting? Maybe an apartment or condo would be a better idea since you're still newly in a relationship."

"That's what I said and now he's mad." Rhi sat down on a bench.

"You're sure he's upset? He told you that?"

Rhi rolled her eyes. "I've lived with him and known him long enough to know when he's mad."

Jackie scoffed. "I've lived with Everett for fifty-one years and still don't know if he's mad at me or upset with himself. This is a big decision. Chances are he's upset with himself for not thinking about it."

"What happens if this doesn't work? I don't know if we could go back to living as friends if it doesn't." Rhi glanced over to where Levi stood near his car.

"Then how is getting an apartment or a condo together any different? If you pay outright for a house, you sell it and go your own ways. With a condo or apartment, you have a lease to break, leaving one of you to pay rent on your own."

"And if he wants to stay in the house and I paid for it?"

"Then he buys the place from you." Jackie took Rhi's hand. "You love him, I know you do. And do you think if your parents or I thought this was a terrible idea, we'd even be involved?"

"I'm sure there's a backup plan in place if it doesn't work out." Rhi chuckled.

Jackie pulled her into an embrace. "Always."

"Are you still willing to show us the other house?"

"Of course, dear, come along." Jackie strolled to her SUV and climbed in.

Rhi bounded over to where Levi stood and bumped his shoulder. "I'm not planning on us not working out. I hope you know that."

"I do. And here I am, trying to talk you into a house when I didn't think about that aspect." Levi kissed her forehead.

"I talked to Aunt Jackie. The house may be the best way to go so we don't have to break leases."

"Did you want to stop looking for today?"

"No, let's go look at this one, then maybe..."

"What?"

"If we don't like this one, what if we talked to Edge about renting his place? We could spend more time looking for our perfect house."

Levi opened the door for Rhi. "He said you could have it. I doubt he'll charge you rent to stay there."

"Would you like me to see if he's home?" Jackie grinned.

"Let's wait until we see this next house."

"It's the blue house two doors over."

Levi climbed into his car and followed Jackie down the street. "It looks nicer than the first one."

"I love the stonework. It reminds me of my parents' house."

"Does it come with your mom's cooking?"

"Nah, but we'd be close enough, so you know she'd bring food over."

"Mom's Delivery Service. I like it."

Rhi hit him in the arm and got out of the SUV.

"This one is a little bigger than the last one. There's a guest apartment over the garage. The master is on the main floor, an office you could turn into a bedroom, and two bedrooms upstairs."

"What are we going to do with all the space?" Rhi stared at the house. It didn't look that big from the outside.

"What would we do with all the room at Edge's place?"

"I don't know. I've always loved his house. Despite its size, it always felt cozy and…homey."

"That may have had something to do with him being there though." Levi grabbed her hand as they walked toward the front door. "Let's see the inside. I'm liking it so far. We could let Robby move into the space over the garage."

"Robby?"

"Your dad said their network administrator is retiring soon and when I talked to Robby about it originally, he said to think of him if I ever have an opening. He's ready to get out of the big city."

"The guest suite at Edge's has a separate entrance. That could work." Rhi nodded.

Jackie smiled. "There's a staircase on the side of the garage leading up to the apartment here. He doesn't even have to enter the house." She opened the door and led them inside.

"Yeah, and if this doesn't work, you can move me up there." Levi chuckled.

They walked through the foyer and into the living room. A fireplace took up a large portion of the wall to the right. The open kitchen was to the left.

"There's plenty of room for entertaining." Levi turned around in the living area.

"And I love the fireplace."

"Out this door is a covered back porch with an outdoor fireplace and kitchen."

"I'm not sure we need the outdoor kitchen, but the outside fireplace reminds me of the island." Levi glanced out the back door.

"That makes me wonder if Edge's house would be better for us. The whole house reminds me of the island. And they have the same wicker outdoor furniture on their patio." Rhi glanced around. "How much bigger is Edge's house than this one?"

Jackie pulled out her phone. "Looks like this one is just a tad smaller than his. Same number of bedrooms. The kitchen in Edge's house is larger. He has the media room upstairs. Plus his basement."

"Oh, I forgot about the media room. Why go to the movies when we can bring the theater to our friends?" Levi beamed.

"If we head back to the front, this is the home office."

"I love the window seating, but is that enough to justify spending this much money on a house?"

Levi wrapped his arm around her waist. "The office is almost in the same place at Edge's. We could add a window seat."

"Was that office big for us to share though?"

"I figured I'd take one of the rooms in the basement. Remember when we were in high school and he'd let us play video games in his work room? Do you know how nice it would be to see my software designs in that much detail? I could finally finish that video game I've been working on."

"Sounds like you're leaning more toward his house." Rhi turned to face him.

"I like the idea of both of us having our own spaces. We're going to be sharing a bedroom for the first time ever. I know over the years I've pissed you off enough for you to need your own space and you're the one that will be working from home. With that space, I'll have the option to go into the office or work from home."

Rhi hugged him. "What kind of understanding boyfriend knows a girl needs space?"

"The kind that's lived with you for five years and knows how scary you can be at times." He chuckled.

She smacked him on the shoulder. "I like this place, but I think you're right about Edge's."

"Let's go over to Edge's."

Chapter Thirty-One

Levi

JUNE 16TH

Levi walked up to the front door of Edge's house.

The door opened, and Edge waved the three of them in.

"I'm going to make a couple phone calls while you three hash things out." Jackie motioned back to her vehicle.

"You mean you're not going to come in and see me, Aunt Jackie? I'm insulted." Edge's smile betrayed his fake outrage.

"I'm sorry you're insulted, but I lose my commission if you give them the house." Jackie winked.

"I'll sell it to them for a dollar so you can get commission." He laughed.

"Now who's insulted?" Jackie gave a mock scoff and turned back to the SUV. "I'll see you Sunday morning."

"Well of course you are. I'm trying to talk half your kids into moving to Minnesota."

Jackie gave a sad nod. "I'm not sure it will take much convincing. Everett and I have been talking about a retirement-slash-family vacation home up there but were going to wait a few more years. That might have to happen sooner rather than later now. And in the meantime, it's a good thing we have a private plane."

"How many of the family are you gonna convert to residents of the great white North?" Levi chuckled.

"No one who doesn't want to come willingly." Edge shut the door behind them. "I'm happy to leave this off the market if you want to just live here until you find a place."

"We're actually kinda thinking this may be where we want to live. We've been talking about it all morning, and everything seems to lead back to here." Levi put his arm around Rhi.

"Oh yeah?" Edge motioned to the living room. "I'd ask if you want the whole tour, but I think you've been here a time or two."

"I'll give you market value for it. I've always loved this place, and I'd really hate the idea of you selling it."

"Why? You're my sister and part of me doesn't want to sell. If I give it to you, I can stay here when I'm in town visiting." Edge shrugged and stuffed his hands in his pockets.

Rhi frowned. "If you don't want to get rid of it, we can stay here as caretakers until we find another place."

"I have no problem signing it over to you. I would love to do that. The idea of selling it to someone outside the family felt very...final. There are a lot of memories in this house. And even though I have no desire to move back to Indiana, there's always a piece of me that will call this home."

"Are you getting sentimental on us now?" She narrowed her eyes then winked.

"Yeah. I'm actually getting ready to tell Mom that Sara's pregnant again, so there's definitely a bit of sentimentality here." Edge smiled.

"She is? I'm going to have another niece or nephew?" Rhi threw her arms around his neck.

"Yep, and I'm excited to be able to go through the whole process this time."

"Congratulations. That kinda makes sense why you wouldn't want to sell when you're going through that." Levi shook his hand.

"I know we're going to have to spend more time down here during the pregnancy, and especially after the baby is born, so it would be nice to have a place to stay." Edge chuckled.

"Well, you're welcome any time." Rhi looked around the room. "I always thought this place was too big for two people, but I'm starting to see the benefits to all the space."

"Sara used the office for her work, and the basement was set up with every modern computer system in mind. We always had people over, so it never felt oversized. Well, not until I was alone in it for a few years."

Levi nodded. "I loved your setup down there. Might have to recreate that at some point. Where is Sara?"

"She's visiting her dad."

Levi took Rhi's hand. "Do you mind if we look around?"

"Not at all. Go for it. If you haven't seen the master bedroom, it's right through there." He motioned to the door behind him.

Levi tugged on Rhi's hand as they walked. "What are you thinking?"

"I'm thinking I want this house. I know it's a totally different direction that we had talked about, but it really feels like the right move. What about you?"

"Remembering the basement set up and how much I could get done down there makes me think this is the right choice. There's still a guest suite for Robby if he wants to live here for a while. And there's more than enough space for entertaining."

Rhi took in the master. "I want it."

"We'll have to make our own repairs or hire out."

"We'll hire out for sure. Neither one of us is that handy."

"What if things don't work out?" Levi shoved his hands in his pockets.

"I don't think it's going to be an issue, but if it ever comes to that, I guess I'll buy you out…not that we'll have any money invested in the actual house purchase."

"Except the dollar so Aunt Jackie gets her commission." Levi chuckled and hugged her back.

Rhi nodded. "Let's go let Edge know we want it then find Aunt Jackie."

"Never thought I'd be doing this, but I'm glad it's with my best friend."

June 18th

L evi unlocked their apartment door.

Robby walked down the hall and clapped him on the shoulder. "Hey, man. Back from paradise already?"

"Yep. I could have stayed another week though. I love it down there."

"Party at your place tonight?"

Levi shook his head. He wanted to fall in bed with Rhi, not worry about entertaining anyone but her. "Nah, I'm not in the partying mood."

Robby smacked him in the arm. "I'm sure you were busy with all those island girls following you around." He leaned in close. "How many hearts did you break? Seven? Ten?"

"No broken hearts and I…" He stopped.

"You what? Secret admirer? Sounds like you need to get out. We could head to the bar."

"Actually, Robby, I'm off the market."

Robby cackled. "Dude, if you don't want to hang out

tonight, just tell me. You don't have to make shit up." He shook his head.

Levi glared at Robby. "I'm serious. I'm in a committed relationship."

"With whom? That was way too fast for you to be committed."

"Me." Rhi kissed Levi on the cheek. "We're together now. For the long haul."

Robby's eyes widened. "Seriously?"

Levi nodded and put his arm around Rhi. "Yep. We made the leap while we were gone."

"That's amazing! Congratulations." Robby pulled them both into a hug. "When's the wedding?"

"There's no engagement yet, but we are buying a house together." Levi opened the door to their apartment and motioned Robby inside. "I do want to talk to you about something."

"Sure, what's up?"

"Remember the job I told you about with Rhi's dad?"

"Yeah, the sweet one where you're gonna own the company? I'm telling you, man, if you need a systems administrator, I'll be there in a heartbeat."

"Good, because the one at the company is retiring in a couple months."

Robby sank onto the couch. "You two are pulling my legs, right? I'm drunk or high and you're making all this shit up. When I sober up, it's all going to be one big joke, right?"

Rhi laughed. "Nope, we're serious. The house we're buying has a studio over the garage so you can stay there until you find a place of your own."

Robby's jaw dropped. "I'm in shock. I don't know what to say."

Levi chuckled. "Go back to your place and think about it. It's not like I have the job opening today. You still have time. But we'd love for you to join us. I'll talk to Leon and see what kind of salary we would be offering and we'll go from there."

Robby nodded as he stood. "I mean, I'd love to get out of the place I'm at, so I'm definitely interested. Yeah, get me the salary stuff and I'll put in some serious consideration."

"Great." Levi hugged him.

Robby headed to the door. "Thanks, boss."

Levi shut the door behind him then sat down on the couch. "I'm not, like, a bad guy or anything, am I?"

"No, of course not. Why?"

"I told Robby I was off the market, and he thought I was lying and just didn't want to hang out with him."

"I mean, do you wanna hang out with him when you can be with me?" She plopped down on the couch.

"You win—even when we weren't dating." He wrapped his arms around her. "It was the way he said it. Kinda made me feel like an asshole."

"You've always been a confirmed bachelor. How many times have you said that to me? It'll take our friends longer to think of you as a guy in a relationship."

"I guess you're right." He let out a heavy breath.

"Everyone is going to think that at least once. We've both been serial daters for so long, our friends are bound to be surprised. Even Delilah didn't believe it when I told her."

"True." Levi grinned. "Are you excited to see Edge and Sara this weekend to finalize all the paperwork with Jackie?"

"For sure! That means we need to start packing tomorrow though."

"I was thinking…instead of worrying about whose bed we take with us, we get a new one for the new place."

"Yes. One hundred percent agree with you there." Rhi smiled at him. "I'm excited about the house."

"Me too." He stood and pulled her to her feet.

"Call me crazy, but it's like we were always meant to be together. It just took longer for us to figure it out."

"We met in kindergarten, so it would have been hard for us to recognize the complexities of love then."

Rhi hugged him close. "But even there, we knew. Remember when I told you we'd be friends forever?"

"You're the one with the good memory, but I do remember that."

"I feel like we missed time being with each other because we didn't recognize there were more feelings. No wonder neither of us could keep a relationship."

"I never tried." He kissed her head. "We've been together though. The only thing we missed out on was great sex."

"*Of course* your head goes there."

"Where else would it go? What else have we missed out on? We've taken care of each other when we're sick. We help each other out. We spend time together. And we also took the time to figure out what we didn't want. Sometimes that's more important than the time we may have missed."

Rhi pushed up on her toes and pressed a kiss to Levi's lips. "You're an amazing man, Levi Morris."

"Nah, I'm an asshole who occasionally says the right things."

"I love you. You know that, right?" She ran her fingers through his hair.

"Of course, I do. I love you too."

"I mean like real romantic love. The kind my parents have. The kind Edge and Sara have. Not just friendship love…it's real."

"I repeat. I love you too. In the exact same way."

Epilogue
Rhi

Rhi fell onto the couch in their private villa on Edgerly Island. "It's New Year's Eve, and I'd rather spend the night in bed with you than go to a party."

"Yeah, me too. But your parents are celebrating an anniversary."

"What, the night Edge was conceived?"

Levi's eyes widened. "Did I miss part of this story?"

"Mom and her family were on a vacation to this island over the holidays when Mom was seventeen. She found out she was pregnant a month and a half later."

Levi's face turned a deep shade of red. "Well, they still met around this time, so that could be the anniversary."

"What are you embarrassed about?"

"Nothing. I guess I'd never heard the whole story." Levi glanced at his watch. "I'm going to get ready. We're supposed to be there soon."

Rhi kissed his cheek and followed him into the bedroom. "What are you wearing?"

"Suit." Levi disappeared into the bathroom.

She frowned. Something was up. She picked up the teal dress she'd worn on their first date. If they were going to celebrate firsts, she might as well do the same for them. She went into the other bathroom to fix her makeup and hair. When she returned to their room, there was a note on the bed.

Sara said she'd bring you.
Headed over there. Love you.

Rhi frowned again. She trudged into the living area and found Sara sitting on the couch. "What's going on?"

Sara gave her a broad smile. "I have no idea."

"You're lying."

"Maybe."

Rhi glared at her. "Seriously, I want to know what's up."

"Don't worry about it. You'll find out when you get there. I promise you it's a good surprise." Sara hugged her.

Rhi took a deep breath. "Levi's surprises are usually good things. I wish he wasn't acting so weird."

Sara glanced at her watch and yawned. "I wish they hadn't started this so late. These days, I'm usually asleep by now."

Rhi laughed. "You and me both. But it is New Year's Eve, so you do have to expect things to be late."

"Come on, it's already eleven."

Sara drove the golf cart over to the private family residence on the island. The two of them walked into the main room.

Rhi stopped in her tracks. Robby and some of their

other friends were there. All of her grandparents, Levi's father, and many of her aunts and uncles and cousins from both sides of the family.

She leaned over to Sara. "What's going on?"

"We're all ringing in the New Year." Sara smiled.

"I thought we were celebrating some anniversary for Mom and Dad."

"God, I hope not. That would be Edge's conception and we don't need to give him that kind of comedy ammunition." Sara shook her head.

"You can say that again." Rhi scanned the room for Levi until her gaze met his. She trudged toward him, but her Grandma Laverne stopped her.

"Honey, you are doing the most amazing work with our social media. We're booked solid through next year this time." She hugged Rhi.

"Thanks, Grandma. It's been a lot of fun and I'd love to stay on."

"Oh, that's a definite yes. I wouldn't let that boy fire you if he tried."

"I'm glad. I need to go find Levi."

"Of course, dear." Laverne patted her on the cheek.

Her cousin Manda waved her over next. "You have no idea how much I needed this trip."

Rhi hugged her. "I'm glad you're here. Can you tell me more about why everyone is here though?"

"Nope. Mom just said we were spending the New Years on the island, and I definitely needed the break."

"Have you found anyone yet?"

"No, but Hunter contacted me out of the blue about

three or four months ago. We've been talking a *lot* since then." Manda smiled.

"Hunter? As in Hunter Cross. Superstar country singer. Hunter who we went to school with?"

"The one and only."

"Are you going to meet up with him?"

"The only way I think we'll actually manage to get together is if I go to one of his concerts and hang around afterwards like some groupie, and I just can't." Manda chuckled. "I tried to convince him to meet us all here, but he's on tour and can't get away."

"And that's why I could never date someone who was in the music business. I didn't realize I preferred stability until I figured out Levi was the one for me."

"He has been the one non-family constant for you since kindergarten."

Rhi scanned the room and her gaze landed on Levi and his dad. "Levi's dad is here too? Why do I feel like we're celebrating more than just the New Years?"

Manda shrugged. "I don't know. Mom's waving me over. We'll have to hang out more tomorrow."

"Sounds good. Love you, girl."

"Love you too." Manda headed toward the buffet.

Rhi looked to where she had just seen Levi, but he was gone. She walked across the room, only to be stopped again by Link and Liam. Grandma and Grandpa O'Riley stopped her after that. She found herself talking to a continuous line of family until right before midnight.

Her aunt Sandie glanced down at her watch. "My goodness. It's only one minute to midnight. You better go find your honey."

"I've been trying to do that all night," she muttered as she stalked to the last place she'd seen Levi.

He caught her hand, spun her around, and pulled her into his arms. "Hi."

"What are you hiding from me? And why does it seem like my entire family has kept me from you since I came in here?"

Levi smiled. "It was a bit of a secret, but they're all here for us."

She quirked an eyebrow. "For us? What are you talking about?"

"TEN." The countdown to midnight started.

Rhi looked at her friends and family, all staring at the pair. She turned back to Levi.

"NINE."

He held a diamond solitaire engagement ring in his hand.

"EIGHT."

"Rhi, will you marry me?"

"SEVEN."

"Yes."

"SIX."

Levi slipped the ring on her finger.

"FIVE."

The room erupted in cheers.

"FOUR."

Levi leaned in for a kiss.

"THREE."

Rhi held her lips away from his. "Two," she counted in tandem with everyone else.

"ONE."

Their lips met.

Levi cupped the back of her neck with one hand and pulled her close with the other.

Cheers went up again.

"Happy New Year!"

"Congratulations."

Rhi rested her head against his chest, studying the ring on her finger. "Remember last New Year's?"

"Yeah, I got food poisoning and kicked out the girl I was with shortly after midnight."

"She was lying on the floor throwing the mother of all tantrums because you wouldn't agree to another date with her."

"I believe I was puking at the time."

"Right! I never thought I'd be wearing your ring on my finger a year later."

"Neither did I. But it was on nights like those I should have realized you were my soulmate."

"Oh yeah?"

"Yep. Of all the people who've come in and out of my life, you've always been there for me. You've seen me at my worst, and I've seen you at yours. And we're still here no matter what."

Rhi smiled and kissed his lips. "I love you, Levi."

"I love *you*."

A Note From Ellen & Kindred

Thank you for reading *Not So Suddenly Soulmates*! We hope you enjoyed being a fly on the wall as Rhi and Levi found their forever person. We would greatly appreciate it if you could take a moment to leave a review wherever Kindred books are sold. Your reviews help other bookworms discover similar stories and make informed choices about their reading selections. Your feedback is valuable to us and the literary community.

Acknowledgments

Karan Heitschmidt: You're amazing and I love you and that is all.

About the Author

Ellen Wilder writes realistic romantic fiction novels. Well, realistic minus the abundance of wealthy people, because everyone should have a little fantasy in their lives. She lives in Southwest Minnesota with her own romance hero husband, three kids, one dog, and six cats.

Ellen loves all things Tolkien and Star Wars. She's a nerd at heart and has always been a book worm. She started writing when she was twelve and has been ever since. She loves to write characters with flaws. Characters who are imperfectly perfect, who have mental health issues, and challenge social norms.

Connect with Ellen at ellenwilder.weebly.com.

amazon.com/-/e/B01GT4IOOO
bookbub.com/authors/ellen-wilder
facebook.com/ellenwilder82
instagram.com/ellenwilder82
pinterest.com/ellenwilder82

About the Publisher

Kindred Ink Press publishes fictional stories in a variety of genres for readers of all ages, from those just learning to read, to those who have been reading for decades and still love to devour new stories. Our books range from quick reads to those of epic length and can be found in digital ebook and print formats with audiobooks in the future.

Our mission is to connect readers with authors who write the stories they want to read, stories that take them to another place, stories they want to talk about and read more than once.

Sign up for the Kindred Insider email newsletter to receive new releases, sales, and exclusive content in your inbox!

https://kindredinkpress.com/kindredinsider/

facebook.com/kindredinkpress

tiktok.com/@kindredinkpress

instagram.com/kindredinkpress

pinterest.com/kindredinkpress